'We're being asked to hunt down a guy who saved our lives and kill him, based on some story they've picked up,' said Two Moons.

Mitch didn't have time to answer. There was a sudden explosion, and Gaz's door hurtled towards them in a ball of flame . . .

BOOKS BY JIM ELDRIDGE

Black Ops: Jungle Kill

Black Ops: Death in the Desert

Black Ops: Urban Assassin

BLACK OPS.

URBAN ASSASSIN

JIM ELDRIDGE

EGMONT

To Lynne, for always!

EGMONT

We bring stories to life

Black Ops: Urban Assassin
First published 2011 by Egmont UK Limited
239 Kensington High Street
London W8 6SA

Text Copyright © 2011 Jim Eldridge
All rights reserved

The moral rights of the author have been asserted

ISBN 978 1 4052 5477 9

3 5 7 9 10 8 6 4 2

A CIP catalogue record for this title is available from the British Library

Printed and bound in Great Britain by the CPI Group

1

Mitch was crouched low on the roof wearing Kevlar body armour, night-vision goggles, and cradling an M80 automatic rifle. Tonight, the British Embassy in Istanbul was a battleground for him and the rest of Delta Unit.

Beside Mitch on the roof was Mehmet Koman of MIT. Turkish Intelligence. He was also kitted out in body armour, with night vision and an automatic rifle, as well as other weapons for hand-to-hand fighting: knives, small blades, wire garrottes.

'Think they'll come in via the roof?' Mitch asked Koman in a whisper.

'That's what I'd do,' Koman replied.

Fits our plan perfectly, thought Mitch. The idea was to let the attackers come on to the roof and get inside the Embassy through the rooftop door. Once they were inside, Delta Unit would ambush them. While Mitch and Koman kept watch on the roof, the other five members of the unit were lying in wait inside the building.

'Remember, we'd prefer to take them alive,' Koman told Mitch. Mitch nodded. A dead terrorist was just a body. A captured one could be a goldmine of information.

'Action outside,' whispered Colonel Nelson's voice suddenly through Mitch's earpiece. 'MIT have spotted the targets. They're at the back of the building. Looks like one of them's holding a crossbow.'

'Grappling hooks,' guessed Koman. 'These old buildings are perfect for that, with their ornamental ledges.'

Even as he spoke they heard a clatter from the edge of the roof, not far away from them. A metal barb had landed, a rope attached to the end of it. As they watched the hook was pulled back, and its curved ends caught on the roof's decorative brick surround, exactly as Koman had predicted.

'Let me guess, you've done this yourself,' said Mitch.

Koman smiled. 'Only in training.'

The two men watched as the hook started to take the strain.

'They're on their way up to the roof,' Mitch reported to Nelson through his microphone.

'Copy that,' Nelson responded. 'Let them get through the door into the building. We'll take them once they're in. Stay on the roof in case they try to get back that way.'

'Affirmative,' said Mitch.

Inside the building, Nelson gestured to the others to take up their positions.

'They're on their way,' he said.

Suddenly Two Moons stiffened. 'There's someone outside the rear window! I saw a shadow,' he warned.

'A two-pronged attack.' Tug nodded. 'The roof and the alley.'

'I'll take the stairs,' said Nelson. 'Gaz, you're with me.'

The two soldiers ran to the stairs and took position part-way up, while Tug, Benny and Two Moons took cover behind the heavy filing cabinets, their rifles aimed at the windows overlooking the alley.

'No one moves until they're inside,' whispered Tug.

On the roof, Mitch and Koman crouched down behind the chimney stack. The head of a man appeared over the ornate Turkish parapet as he hauled himself on to the roof. He quickly checked the coast was clear. A bag hung round his neck and a long coil of rope dangled from his shoulders. The man tied one end of the rope to a metal stanchion and dropped the coil over the edge of the roof. There were now two ropes for the attackers to climb up.

Mitch and Koman watched silently as the man hurried over to the access door. The attacker tried the door then pulled out something from the bag slung round his neck. Mitch and Koman heard the whine of a drill.

Koman gave an approving nod. 'Quieter than blowing it, and quicker than trying to pick it. These are professionals.'

While the man worked, more figures were appearing over the edge of the roof. Mitch counted them. Five in total.

'Four coming down to you. One on the roof,' Mitch hissed into his microphone.

From his position on the stairs, Nelson looked across at the rear window. Tug had moved across the room so that he was right beside it.

As Tug watched, he saw the metal security grille across the window being pulled away as the attackers unscrewed the fixings that held it on.

Tug hurried back to join the others. 'They're

good, whoever they are,' he murmured. 'This is a quiet operation.'

'Not for long,' grunted Two Moons, hefting his automatic rifle.

Mitch slid out from his hiding place and began to crawl along the chimney stack, easing his way closer to his target – the man guarding the door. He knew what it was like to be on guard on a roof at night. Every one of your senses was strained to breaking point as you listened for any sound or sudden change that might indicate an attack: the smell of tobacco from a smoker, the scent of hair gel.

Two Moons, Tug and Benny watched the black-clad terrorists prise open the window and climb inside. They waited, ready for action, as the intruders began placing incendiary devices along the walls. It was obvious that once they'd stolen what they were after, they were going to burn the building to get rid of any evidence.

Suddenly the Delta soldiers heard footsteps from the stairs and the four men appeared from the roof. As the first of them made it to the bottom of the stairs, Gaz moved out of the shadows, slamming the butt of his rifle into the man's stomach. The intruders swung their guns towards Gaz, reacting to the sudden movement, but Tug, Benny, Two Moons and Nelson opened fire before they could bring their weapons to bear.

Mitch could see the man on guard clearly now. He was dressed from head to toe in black, a balaclava helmet covering his face and an automatic rifle in his hands. As the gunfire sounded, the man swung towards the open door. Mitch saw his chance. He dived from his hiding place and grabbed the man from behind, wrapping both arms round him, trapping the man's arms to the sides of his body to stop him aiming his rifle. Then Mitch slammed the man forwards, smashing him face first into the solid bricks of the doorway. Mitch felt the man go limp and the rifle dropped from his fingers.

Mitch released the terrorist and he crumpled down, unconscious.

Koman was already at Mitch's side. Swiftly, Koman tied up the unconscious man with strong plastic cables.

The sound of gunfire still raged below them.

'Sounds like they've got trouble,' said Mitch to Koman. Just then Nelson's voice came through his earpiece: 'Two terrorists heading up to the roof.'

Mitch dragged the guard's body out of sight behind a chimney. Then he and Koman took cover once again, rifles aimed at the open doorway. They were barely hidden when two figures burst out. Only one of them had a gun.

Koman stepped out and hit the one with the gun across the face with the butt of his automatic rifle.

The other man didn't hang around. He ran for the edge of the roof where the ropes dangled. Mitch gave chase, sprinting across the uneven surface of the rooftop. Flipping his gun as he ran, Mitch used the rifle as a club, swinging it in an arc and hitting the man at the back of the knee, just as he reached the edge.

Mitch took a second to catch his breath before pointing his rifle at the fallen attacker.

'It's over!' he snapped. 'Vermek yukan!'

He knew his Turkish wasn't perfect, but he hoped the person on the ground would recognise it as 'Give up!'

Instead, the man leapt up and threw himself at Mitch, swinging wild punches as he came to his feet. Mitch stepped back a pace, out of reach, and fired a single shot near the attacker's feet as a warning. It didn't work. The man turned and lunged for the edge of the roof again.

'Oh, no you don't,' shouted Mitch, throwing himself at the man. The force of the collision carried them both to the precipice. For a split second they teetered on the edge, before tumbling out into the air. Mitch saw the ground far below, and the lights of the city streets staring up at him as he fell. He reached out with one hand and managed to grab the top of the stone parapet. With his other hand he still had hold of the attacker's clothing.

Pain coursed through his shoulder socket. The strain on his arms was pulling at every muscle fibre. The attacker kicked and struggled, making Mitch's job even harder.

I can't hold on for much longer, he thought.

'Let him fall!' shouted Koman from above.

'You wanted him alive!' Mitch yelled back.

There was a sudden shot. The attacker stopped struggling and went limp.

'He's dead now!' Koman snapped, holding his pistol at his side. 'Let him fall.'

Mitch looked down at the terrorist, saw the blood dripping from his skull. He released his grip and the body plummeted to the ground far below.

Koman reached down, grabbed hold of Mitch and helped him clamber back on to the roof.

'So much for taking them alive,' Mitch grunted as he lay on the cold, hard surface, his breaths coming in ragged gasps.

'We have those two,' said Koman, gesturing across the roof towards the doorway, where the other men lay, tied up.

In his ear Mitch heard Nelson say: 'All clear down here. Interior of building secured. Four casualties, two prisoners.'

'Roof secured,' reported Mitch, clambering to his feet. 'Two prisoners. One casualty.' He sighed and added: 'He's down in the street. You'd better get MIT to clear up the mess.'

2

The soldiers of Delta Unit regrouped and headed for their vehicles, parked just outside the British Embassy. Koman and the other members of MIT had taken away the bodies of the dead attackers, and the prisoners.

'Now that's what I call a successful operation,' said Two Moons as they walked.

'Half of them are dead,' Mitch pointed out.

'Yeah, but we all came out alive!' Two Moons grinned.

'Good job, guys,' said Nelson. 'The Turkish authorities will be very happy. Looks like we stopped that terrorist plot.'

Suddenly Nelson's pager went off. They all turned as Nelson scanned it. The colonel's face hardened.

'It's a Code 9,' he told them grimly.

Code 9 was the signal that recalled Delta Unit back
to their base in London for an emergency situation.
It was a good hour drive to the NATO air base, just
outside Istanbul, and by the time they pulled into
the military compound Mitch and the rest of the
unit were exhausted. Nelson tried contacting HQ
to get more details. All he was promised was that
they would be given all the information when they
arrived back in the UK.

At the air base they boarded a small military
jet. No customs, no protocol, just straight on to the
plane and then take-off for Northolt RAF base, just
outside London.

'It can't be that urgent,' argued Gaz, 'or they'd
bring in a unit that's nearer. Let's face it, we're in
Turkey. There are two other units in the UK, plus a
couple in Germany and one in Norway.'

'I guess there's a reason it has to be us,'
mused Tug.

'You think we're in trouble?' asked Two Moons. 'We're going back for a court-martial or something?'

Mitch shook his head. 'Code 9 means a real emergency situation. Something big's going down that they need us to deal with.'

The plane journey was fast and noisy. As they disembarked at Northolt, they were met by a small man in a neat dark suit, and a uniformed army captain.

'Colonel Nelson, I need you to come with me,' said the suited man. Turning to the rest of Delta Unit, he told them, 'Captain Lawrence and his men will escort you back to your base at Regent's Park. Colonel Nelson will be rejoining you shortly.' He gestured towards two military vehicles parked near the runway. Behind them was a small helicopter.

Suddenly Mitch realised that the man in the suit was an Intelligence agent.

We're in spy territory, he thought.

'I'll see you guys later,' said Nelson, and he followed the agent, who was now running towards the waiting helicopter. This is a real emergency, thought Mitch.

Nelson and the man got into the helicopter which took off almost immediately. The rest of Delta Unit followed Captain Lawrence towards the military vehicles and as Mitch and Two Moons climbed into the first vehicle, Two Moons muttered: 'You thinking what I'm thinking?'

'Spooks?' murmured Mitch. 'Either MI5 or MI6.'

'Bingo!' said Two Moons.

Three hours later the squad were in the briefing room at their base in Regent's Park. Coffee, sandwiches and doughnuts sat on the tables in front of them, but there was no sign of Colonel Nelson, nor any word from the USUKCSF High Command on where he was or how soon he'd be back.

Mitch studied his friends and reflected again on how lucky he was to have been brought into Delta Unit. He'd been on the outside – kicked out of the SAS after killing his corrupt senior officer – when

Colonel Nelson had offered him the chance to join the unit on a special mission.

He had proved himself invaluable and now he was a core member of the six-man team: three Americans, three Brits.

They were a young and mixed bunch: Colonel Chuck Nelson, the tall black Bostonian, in charge of the Unit; his second in command, Captain Robert 'Tug' Tait, the son of a British Lord; Lieutenant Benny Jaurez, a Latino Texan, the unit's tactician; Sergeant Tony Two Moons, the tall Sioux Native American; Trooper Gaz Graham, the short and stocky Geordie from Newcastle; and Trooper Paul Mitchell, known to everyone as Mitch.

'The guy in the suit said the colonel would be rejoining us shortly,' muttered Two Moons as he munched on a doughnut.

'Yeah, but he was a spook,' said Mitch. 'Spooks lie for a living. Never believe anything they tell you.'

'Not even the ones on our side?' asked Two Moons.

'*Especially* the ones supposedly on our side,' said Mitch.

Tug's mobile rang. 'It's Nelson,' he told the others. He answered the call and listened briefly, then said: 'Fine. We'll see you.'

Tug hung up and turned to the others. 'The colonel's on his way. He says he'll be here in about twenty minutes.'

'Where was he?' Benny asked.

'It sounded like he was in a car so my guess is he's been somewhere in London.'

'Somewhere with a helipad.' Benny nodded thoughtfully.

'Guess we'll find out soon enough,' said Two Moons. He pointed at the two remaining doughnuts. 'Anyone else want those?'

'You bet!' said Gaz, grabbing one.

'Me too,' said Benny, snatching up the other.

Two Moons looked at his two friends indignantly as they stuffed the doughnuts into their mouths.

17

'Huh, that's what I get for being polite!' He scowled jokingly. 'Next time I'm just gonna eat 'em!'

It was half an hour before Nelson walked in. He was carrying a laptop under his arm.

'Sorry to keep you waiting, fellas,' he said. 'The briefing took a while. Then there was traffic.'

'Is it a Code 9?' asked Benny.

Nelson nodded. 'Yep. By my definition, this classes as an emergency all right.' He put the laptop on the table and connected it to the Power-Point display unit. He pressed a few keys, and on the screen on the wall appeared a title card that said, '*G20 Conference and Treaty on Terrorist Extradition.*'

'This is what it's all about, guys. And it opens here in London in just five days' time.'

The others exchanged puzzled looks.

'It's a conference,' said Gaz. 'Politicians talking. How does that affect us?'

'I guess it must be the subject matter,' murmured Tug. 'Terrorist Extradition.'

'Dead right, Tug,' Nelson replied. 'All the G20 nations are coming to London to sign a treaty which will mean that terrorist suspects arrested in one country can be extradited to another country quickly and without lengthy appeals.'

'I thought a treaty like that already existed,' said Two Moons.

'To an extent,' agreed Nelson. 'But only a few countries have signed up to it. This one is going to be signed by *all* the members of the G20, including the President of the European Union.'

'So, everyone's on-board to stop terrorists hiding across borders,' Two Moons said in approval. 'A good thing. But I still don't see where we come in.'

'Both MI6 and the CIA have picked up intel that there's to be an assassination attempt during the conference, before the treaty can be signed.'

'Who's the target?' asked Mitch.

'The British prime minister,' said Nelson.

19

The five soldiers sat up, suddenly on high alert.

'Why him?' demanded Gaz.

'Because he's the one who's been pushing for this particular treaty to be signed,' said Nelson. 'The people giving the orders must hope that getting rid of him will kill off the treaty, and send a message to all the other world leaders.'

Benny shook his head. 'I can see why this is an emergency all right, but I still don't see what this has to do with us,' he said.

'We've been given the job of finding the assassin and stopping him,' said Nelson.

The five soldiers exchanged puzzled looks.

'Isn't that rather unusual?' asked Tug. 'Normally stuff like this is a job for the spooks at MI5 or MI6.'

'Usually it would be,' agreed Nelson. 'But this isn't just any assassin.'

A new image appeared on the screen: a head-and-shoulders photo of a young man with a cocky grin on his face. A shocked gasp from Two Moons made Mitch look round.

'What?' he asked.

'It's Jimmy,' said Two Moons, obviously stunned.

'Jimmy?'

'Jimmy Deacon,' said Gaz quietly. 'He's our buddy.'

'He was never my buddy,' growled Benny.

'He was part of the unit,' snapped back Two Moons. 'He was one of us.'

'*Was*,' emphasised Benny. 'Now it seems he's a renegade killer.'

'Let's leave all that till later and get back to the immediate problem,' said Nelson sharply, bringing them to order.

They turned their attention back to the screen. The head and shoulders shot had been replaced by more pictures of the same man in a variety of disguises. In some, he was immediately recognisable as the same young soldier. In others his hair had changed: sometimes long, sometimes dark, then blond, and in one he was completely bald. The clothes he wore varied, too: tribal costumes, smart business suits, a construction worker's outfit. In some he wore glasses, in others not. Sometimes he had a beard or moustache. In a few his cheeks had been stuffed out to make his face fatter.

'This guy's a chameleon,' muttered Mitch.

'That was always his thing,' Gaz said, nodding. 'He loved to use the element of surprise. He could get almost anywhere by changing his appearance.'

'Which is the problem we have,' said Nelson. 'The spooks admit they don't know where or how he'll strike, or what he's going to look like. The only people who stand a chance are those who've worked with him, which is all of us in this room with the exception of Mitch.'

Two Moons shook his head. 'Just because we worked with him don't mean we'll spot him,' he said. 'Like Gaz says, Jimmy was a real master of camouflage. He could walk in anywhere, impossible to spot until it was too late. The guy was a genius.' Two Moons' expression hardened. 'He was also our friend. I don't like this job.'

'It's not up to us to choose whether we like it or not,' said Nelson. 'The intel tells us that Jimmy's going to try to assassinate the British prime minister during this conference and we're the only ones who have a chance of spotting him and stopping him.'

'Maybe the spooks are wrong?' suggested Gaz. 'They've been wrong before.'

'Yes, we know spooks can make mistakes,' Nelson agreed. 'But this seems pretty concrete. It's not just coming from MI6, it's CIA, plus the French and the Germans. It seems that Jimmy's been working renegade for some time, carrying out hits. It's just been lucky for us he hasn't strayed into our territory so far. Now he has, and we've got to stop him.' Nelson checked his watch. 'We've got a briefing at Spook Central in an hour. They're gonna fill us in on everything they've got on Jimmy.' He grinned. 'Believe me, you guys are getting a real privilege here. You've all been given special clearance, but you've got to sign these.' He handed out a sheet of paper to each member of the unit.

'What is this?' asked Two Moons, looking at it suspiciously.

'Official Secrets Act,' explained Nelson. 'If you tell anyone else what you see today, you get shot for treason.'

'I ain't a Brit,' muttered Two Moons. 'They can't shoot me for treason.'

'Yes, they can,' said Nelson. 'If you look closely at the small print, this is a joint UK-US operation.' He grinned again. 'So the Brits shoot their boys, we Yanks shoot you.'

Two Moons shrugged. 'Sounds fair, I guess,' he said. He held out his hand. 'Anyone got a pen?'

3

Once inside MI6 HQ, the men of Delta Unit went through a series of security procedures including retinal scans to verify their individual IDs. Finally they made it to the inner hub where the action took place. They'd been escorted all the way by two men dressed in smart suits. One of them, who introduced himself as Gerald, chatted to the squad as he led them along the corridors, deep inside the building. The other man walked silently just a few paces behind them, keeping a close eye on the unit.

Many of the rooms had glass walls so the soldiers could see inside as they passed. Every room was filled with people at computer terminals, many of them wearing headsets. The walls were adorned with digital maps showing trouble hotspots, red lights flashing on and off highlighting locations.

They're listening in on everyone, thought Mitch. But they still need us to find this man – shows just how good Jimmy Deacon must be.

'Here we are,' said Gerald, pushing open a glass door and ushering them into a room smaller than the ones they'd passed. It looked like a conference room: a long table was set out in the middle, with chairs around it, and a screen on the wall at one end set up for a PowerPoint display. 'Please, take your seats.'

The six soldiers sat down. Gerald went to the laptop at the far end of the table. His silent companion took his place by the door. Mitch noticed the telltale bulge just by the man's arm where he kept his gun.

Mitch looked around the room. Cameras were set in the walls and ceiling, trained on them from every angle. There'll be microphones as well, he thought, and they'll be picking up every word we say. And quite likely a lip-reader somewhere outside, watching the screens, to pick up any comments that don't reach the mikes.

He looked round at the rest of Delta Unit. Like him, they'd settled down on to the chairs and were looking at the screen, taking it all in, not fazed by their surroundings. It was just another mission, but security was tighter than usual. In this world of Secret Intelligence they were outsiders. Suspects to be watched closely.

Gerald pressed a key on the laptop, and a familiar picture appeared on the screen.

'James Deacon,' announced Gerald. 'Your former colleague in Delta Unit, invalided out of the service 18 months ago after suffering severe wounds while on operation with you.'

'He got blown up working for his country,' said Two Moons, a note of defensiveness in his voice. 'He's on our side.'

Gerald shook his head. 'He *was* on our side,' he said smoothly. 'Since he recovered from his wounds, he's been acting as an independent operative.' The photo of Deacon vanished and was replaced by photos of six men, all middle-aged or elderly. A number was on each picture. 'These six have been assassinated by Deacon in the last twelve months. Number one was a British industrialist based in the Bahamas. Fingers in many pies, lots of them suspicious. Deacon was hired by a rival gang to take him out.

'Number two is the former president of a small African state. Officially he died from natural causes. But we have evidence to suggest that Deacon assassinated him using a lethal dose of a narcotic.'

'How did he get close enough to manage that?' asked Tug. 'Most of these politicians are paranoid about letting anyone near them except their very closest cronies.'

'Exactly,' said Gerald. 'That's why we're showing you these – so you can see just how good Deacon is.'

The pictures of the six men vanished from the screen.

'There's no need for me to go into the rest of the

cases,' said the spy. 'It's enough for you to know that these six men are dead, all at Deacon's hands, despite having the most incredible protection and security around them.'

'How is one man able to do all this on his own?' asked Benny.

'He doesn't,' said Gerald.

Another series of shots appeared on the screen. Even without the uniforms Mitch would have been able to tell what these men did for a living. Special Forces soldiers. There was something in their faces: Hard men, trained to kill. Trained to succeed in any circumstances. From the insignia on the collars of their uniforms it was clear that they came from a variety of nations.

'Deacon hires other former Special Forces soldiers as mercenaries for his operations,' said Gerald. 'It seems he puts together a hand-picked team for every operation he leads.'

'How many on each team?' asked Benny.

'That depends on the target,' answered Gerald.

'From what we can gather, sometimes it's four, sometimes six. If it's a particularly hard target, he has been known to use up to eight, but never more than that.'

Mitch nodded. The bigger the team, the more difficult it was to keep control.

'Why haven't you been able to stop him so far?' asked Nelson. 'In cases like this, there has to be a money trail. Follow the money, you find Deacon.'

Again, the Intelligence officer shook his head. 'He's too clever for that. All payments are in cash, so there's no money trail. We usually get a rough idea of where the original payment comes from, but only after the event, when things fall into place.'

'But not in this case?' asked Mitch.

'But not in this case, Mr Mitchell,' agreed Gerald. 'For once, we are ahead of the game. We have intelligence that the money for this operation is being paid from South America. That doesn't necessarily mean the people behind it are South American, of course – it might just be a convenient place to move money from. But we also received a tip-off on where this money was going.'

'A tip-off from who?' asked Mitch. Even as he asked the question, he knew what the answer would be.

'Need to know, Mitch,' said Nelson, beating Gerald to it.

'Yeah, but in this case I think we *do* need to know,' persisted Mitch. 'For all we know, this story is a fake and your informant is winding you up in exchange for some ready cash.'

Gerald shook his head. 'I appreciate your comments, Mr Mitchell, but we are pretty confident about the intelligence we've received.' He hesitated, then said: 'Without going into details, we have an agent operating *inside* the organisation in South America, whose job has been to keep an eye on money transactions. Believe me, we can trust this information.'

'So, you're suggesting Deacon's assembled a team for this operation?' asked Benny.

Gerald nodded.

'Who are they?' asked Tug.

Gerald gave a sigh. 'I'm afraid we don't have that information yet,' he admitted. 'But we have promises of information from our counterparts in Europe and elsewhere; particularly France and South Africa. We believe they have some very strong leads and we hope to have information from them shortly. As soon as we do, you'll know.'

4

After the session at Spook Central, the men of Delta Unit went their separate ways. Tug had arranged to meet his parents, Lord and Lady Tait, at their town house in Kensington; Nelson and Benny both had private business of their own. Mitch, Two Moons and Gaz watched them as they walked off.

'I betcha Benny's private business involves a girlfriend,' commented Two Moons.

'A girlfriend?' echoed Gaz.

'I happen to know that Benny has a girlfriend called Sally who lives in Battersea, and he goes to see her whenever he's in London,' Two Moons said.

'I thought he had a girlfriend in Texas.' Mitch frowned.

'He does!' confirmed Two Moons. 'And if they

ever meet up, boy is he gonna be in trouble.'

'What about the colonel?' asked Gaz. 'He got a girlfriend, too?'

'I never ask questions about his private life,' said Two Moons.

'You know about Benny's though,' pointed out Gaz.

'That's different,' said Two Moons. 'Benny himself told me in confidence.'

'And now you've told us,' said Mitch.

'Which proves one thing to you two guys,' said Two Moons solemnly. 'You should never tell me anything you want to keep a secret.'

Mitch laughed. 'You're supposed to be a comrade! Comrades look out for one another, whatever the situation!'

'Yeah,' said Two Moons, 'that's what comrades do.' His tone had suddenly altered. The humour was gone and he looked serious.

Mitch looked at Gaz, and saw that he also had a concerned look on his face.

'What's the matter?' Mitch asked.

Two Moons and Gaz both looked like they were about to speak, then they hesitated, as if they weren't quite sure how to broach the subject. It was Two Moons who finally spoke.

'You doin' anything right now, Mitch?' he asked.

'No,' said Mitch.

'Then you fancy having a cup of coffee with me and Gaz?'

'Sure,' nodded Mitch. 'Where?'

'Somewhere we can talk in private without being overheard,' said Two Moons. 'I was thinking of Gaz's place.'

'Why mine?' demanded Gaz.

'Because I ain't got me a proper place in this country,' said Two Moons. 'Just a poky little bedsit, and my room at the barracks. At your place the three of us could sit and talk without feeling like sardines in a tin.'

Mitch studied his surroundings as the three soldiers sat in Gaz's living room. No matter how neat and careful Gaz was about his weapons and his equipment, he was very different when he was at home. Clothes had been abandoned on the backs of chairs. There was an empty pizza box poking out from under the settee. A pile of washing filled the small table. It reminded Mitch of his own bedroom as a teenager.

Two Moons ignored the mess, he was too intent on venting his feelings to Mitch.

'The truth is, Mitch, me and Gaz don't feel right about this business with Jimmy Deacon,' said Two Moons.

'He was our pal,' added Gaz. 'And now we're being asked to kill him.'

'That happens in war,' said Mitch. 'Friends and family can end up on opposite sides.'

'This isn't just a case of being on opposite sides,' insisted Two Moons. 'You saw those photos that spook guy, Gerald, showed us of the guys Jimmy hit: A gangster. Some dictator. Hell, those are the guys we take out all the time! That's what we're supposed to do!'

'But we don't do it for money,' pointed out Mitch.

'We get paid,' countered Two Moons.

Mitch laughed. 'There's a bit of a difference between what we get paid as soldiers, and what Jimmy's picking up for hits like these,' he said. 'And this one's the British prime minister. You saying he's a fair target?'

Two Moons shook his head. 'No, of course not,' he said. 'I'm just wondering if they got it right. OK, Jimmy hit these other guys, the crooks. But just because he did that it doesn't mean he's the one behind this.'

'You work with a guy for long enough and you get to know him,' continued Gaz, nodding in agreement. 'Jimmy wasn't that kind of bloke. Headstrong, a bit wild, but nothing dangerous. Not to us, anyway.'

'And he saved our lives,' said Two Moons. 'Me and Gaz's.'

Mitch looked at him, curious.

'It was in South America,' said Gaz. 'We were

on a mission, trying to stop these rebels killing civilians and taking hostages.' He grimaced at the memory. 'Me and Two Moons got separated from the rest of the unit, and were caught by about half a dozen of the rebels. They dragged us to this clearing in the jungle and made us kneel down, hands on our heads.'

Two Moons shook his head at the memory. 'They were all armed to the teeth,' he said. 'Two of them had automatic rifles pointed straight at us. One touch on those triggers and we'd have been blown to bits. They were just about to pump us full of bullets when suddenly Jimmy bursts out of the jungle and *Pop! Pop!* takes out the two guys who are about to shoot us and then fires a burst at the others. All six of them dead within seconds.' Two Moons shook his head. 'Guy saves your life like that, it makes you look at him in a different way, know what I mean. There's a bond between you.'

Mitch nodded. He knew what Two Moons meant. But Two Moons wasn't finished yet.

'We're being asked to hunt down a guy who saved our lives and kill him, based on some story they've picked up.'

'The story's from more than one source,' said Mitch.

'That's what they said about the weapons of mass destruction in Iraq,' said Two Moons. 'Turns out all the sources picked it up from the same place.'

Gaz got up. 'I'm making myself another coffee,' he said. 'You guys want some?'

Mitch and Two Moons didn't have time to answer. There was a sudden explosion, and Gaz's bedroom door hurtled towards them in a ball of flame.

5

The three soldiers instinctively dropped to the floor, the flying door missing them by inches before it crashed into the living room window. As shards of glass rained down on them, Gaz acted swiftly. He snatched up a fire extinguisher and sprayed foam on the burning door before the flames could catch hold of the rest of the flat.

Mitch and Two Moons had leapt to their feet and they quickly checked the rest of the apartment for explosives or a sign of an attacker. There were none.

The explosion had caused panic throughout Gaz's apartment block, and his phone was already ringing. Gaz ignored it while he finished making sure the fire was well and truly out. Then the soldiers heard sirens and saw the blue flashing lights of fire engines and the police drawing up in the street outside.

'Someone's called 999,' said Mitch.

Two Moons shook his head. 'That sure is some fast response,' he said, suspiciously.

'Exactly,' agreed Mitch. 'That call must have been made before the explosion. I think someone is sending us a message.'

It took a while to deal with the firefighters and police. It looked as if there was going to be a whole load of paperwork for Mitch, Gaz and Two Moons to fill out, but then Gerald the Intelligence officer turned up, flashed a card at the Chief Fire Officer and the police officers, and they all left, no questions asked.

Nelson arrived soon after.

The five men stood in Gaz's flat looking at the smouldering door on the floor.

'This is a warning from Deacon,' said Gerald.

'You don't know that!' snapped Two Moons.

'Who else could it be?' asked Gerald.

41

Two Moons looked angry. 'Could be anybody!' he said defensively. 'We've upset a lot of people in our time.'

'I haven't!' protested Gaz.

'Anyway, how come you're here so quickly?' asked Two Moons suspiciously. 'You got someone watching us?'

Gerald shook his head. 'No,' he said, 'but we do monitor all emergency calls. When we spotted that one of the calls was about an explosion at one of Delta Unit's flats, it seemed obvious that it had to be connected.'

'Jimmy could have killed you, Gaz,' said Mitch. 'If you'd been in your room when that bomb went off . . .'

'If it *was* Jimmy!' argued Two Moons.

Nelson was kneeling down beside the burnt door, examining it. 'I don't think this was meant to kill you,' he said. He pointed to the residue on the other side of the door. 'There was just a tiny amount of plastic stuck there, with some paint thinner sprayed on the door to make the explosion look more spectacular.' He used a pen to lift up the burnt remains of a small battery fixed to a piece of thin wire. The end of the wire was still stuck to the door.

'Remote control trigger.' Mitch nodded.

'OK, now I feel better,' said Two Moons. 'He set it off, but made sure we weren't near it when he did.'

Mitch looked at Two Moons and frowned. 'You finding excuses for him?' he asked. 'He blew up Gaz's door. It could have set fire to the flat. We could have been killed.'

Two Moons shook his head. 'No,' he said. 'If it was Jimmy and he'd wanted us dead, we'd be dead. This was just him warning us off, telling us to stay out of his business.'

'So you admit that he's the assassin,' said Mitch.

Two Moons fell silent, but he looked very uncomfortable.

'Get your loyalties straight, Two Moons,' said Nelson quietly. 'Stopping the assassination of the leader of one of our countries, that's *our* business.'

Gaz had been looking gloomily at the blackened door, the smashed window, and the scorched areas of carpet.

'Why did he choose my flat to blow up?' he asked.

'It wouldn't surprise me to find he's done the same where the rest of you live as well,' said Gerald. 'Then he'd have had all bases covered, wherever you'd gone.'

'If he was watching us, he must have had some sort of surveillance in place,' said Gaz. He looked around at the room.

'Don't worry, we'll have it swept for bugs,' said Gerald. He looked at Two Moons, Nelson and Mitch. 'We'd also like permission to check your places.'

'Go ahead.' Nelson nodded.

Mitch hesitated. He didn't like people poking around his flat. But then, what the hell, these were spooks. They'd do it anyway.

'OK,' he said. Two Moons nodded as well.

Just then Gerald's phone rang. 'Yes?' he said

as he put the phone to his ear. He listened for a few seconds, then said: 'We'll be right along.' He hung up and turned to the soldiers. 'That intel I mentioned about the rest of Deacon's team,' he said. 'It's arrived sooner than we expected. They've got it at HQ. I suggest we go and see exactly who you're up against.'

6

They were back at the MI6 HQ within the hour. Tug and Benny were already there, waiting. Tug seemed very amused when Nelson told them about the explosion at Gaz's.

'A burning door!' He grinned. 'That sounds pretty dramatic! Wish I'd seen it!'

'I don't see how it's funny,' protested Gaz. 'It's my door!'

Mitch steered Benny away out of earshot. 'You seem to be the only one who doesn't have a lot of time for Jimmy Deacon,' he said quietly.

'Right,' agreed Benny. He shot a glance at the rest of Delta Unit, who were still talking. 'Even after what happened, and even though they got to admit that he's our assassin, Two Moons is still defending him. And Gaz is more upset about his burnt door than the fact that Deacon nearly killed him.'

'They reckon that Deacon wasn't trying to kill us, just send a warning,' said Mitch.

Benny shook his head. 'Those guys are great, but they can be fools as well,' he said. 'Yeah, Deacon saved their lives. I accept that. But, hell, that's what we all do for one another. You want my opinion?'

Mitch nodded.

'OK. If you ask me, Jimmy Deacon was a selfish show-off who pretended to be a loyal member of the team, but he wasn't. He fooled 'em. He was always a loner rather than a team player – that's why I'm not surprised to find out what he's been doing since he left us. Working as a hit man is much more his style.'

Mitch shot another look at his pals, still talking, then asked Benny quietly, 'You think the debt they feel they owe Jimmy will affect how they handle this operation?'

Benny looked uncertain. 'I hope not,' he said.

'But there's always that sense of loyalty to someone who saved your life in battle. You can't shake it off easy. Know what I mean?'

'I do,' said Mitch, looking at the members of Delta Unit who had become like brothers to him. 'Anyway, you won't have any objections if I kill Deacon?'

'None at all,' agreed Benny. 'We're on one side, he's on the other. And he chose to be on that side. In my opinion, if we don't kill him, he's gonna kill us.'

A voice came from across the room. 'Gentlemen!'

It was Gerald, calling their attention. 'If you will join me in the briefing room, we can show you what we have learnt in the last few hours.'

The soldiers of Delta Unit sat around the table as before. Gerald stood by the laptop overseeing the display, and another man stood guarding the door.

'There are three of them,' announced Gerald. 'All known mercenaries. Two recently arrived in the UK and the third is due to arrive at Heathrow today.

As far as we know, none of them have worked on an operation with Deacon before, but we have sightings of all of them meeting with Deacon in France within the last month.'

He clicked a key and a man's face appeared on the screen. His head was shaved, his nose had been broken at some point, and there was a chunk missing from one of his ears. He looked like a very tough rugby player.

'This is Dmitri Pavel,' announced Gerald. 'Ex-Russian Special Forces, Spetsnatz. He arrived in Britain last week. He escaped the Russian forces and vanished before he could be court-martialled.'

'For what?' asked Tug.

Gerald glanced down at his notes. 'He seems to have quite a list of allegations against him: murder, assault, theft, robbery, treason.' He looked up at the screen. 'Mr Pavel is quite the hard case.' He looked around the table. 'You'll each be getting a more detailed file on these men after this meeting.'

The picture of the Russian vanished to be

replaced by another equally tough-looking man.

'Jan der Smitt: South African,' announced Gerald. 'Former Special Forces, lately working as mercenary to anyone who'll hire him. He's wanted in South Africa and Australia for murder. He's the one due to arrive later today.'

The picture of Smitt vanished, and now a very different one filled the screen. This man had the same shaven head as the previous two, but he was smiling, instead of glaring at the camera. There was something cocky about him.

'Pierre Lavall, ex-French Special Forces,' said Gerald. 'Specialist in explosives. Like Pavel he's been here for just under a week. He can rig a mammoth explosion that'll demolish a building, or a very small one designed to take out a security system. It seems likely that he was the one who rigged your bedroom door, Mr Graham.'

'In that case I've got a score to settle with him,' muttered Gaz.

The Intelligence officer pushed a key on the

laptop and the screen cleared. 'As we've said, Deacon is very elusive, exceptionally hard to pin down. However, we know where these three are and they're under surveillance. It's our hope that one of them will lead us to Deacon.

'So, we have arranged for you to work in three teams of two. Colonel Nelson will sort out who goes with who. As this is an MI6 operation, each team will be accompanied by an MI6 operative; and that MI6 operative will be in charge of the team out in the field.'

The members of Delta Unit turned to look at Colonel Nelson to see how he would react to this. All of them were thinking the same thing: we're soldiers, not spies. We don't want spies giving us orders when it's a matter of life and death.

Nelson looked back at them. 'Sorry, guys,' he said. 'This one's out of my hands. When Gerald here told me what he had in mind, I got straight on to Washington to register a protest. But they say the authority for this operation comes from the very highest. We're talking White House and Whitehall here, and they take precedence over the military. They're our Commanders in Chief. What they say, goes.'

'I assume we'll have control over what weapons we can use in the field?' asked Tug.

'Yes,' said Gerald. 'But within reason. We have to think of the safety of the public. We have to make sure that any weapons you use are . . . proportionate.'

'Yeah, well, I *was* thinking of using a nuclear warhead,' growled Two Moons.

Gerald gave him a short scowl, not amused.

'I don't think you have any need to worry about us and our weapons,' Nelson assured the spy. 'We've all been on missions in civilian situations, so we're aware of what's appropriate and what isn't.'

'Good.' Gerald nodded curtly. 'In that case, please follow me to the canteen, where you will meet your team leaders.'

7

As they left the briefing room, Nelson tapped Mitch and Benny on the shoulders. Two Moons, Gaz and Tug walked on, following Gerald towards the canteen.

'Mitch, I'm putting you with Two Moons. Benny, you'll be with Gaz,' Nelson said quickly and quietly. 'You can guess the reason. I'm worried that Two Moons and Gaz still seem unconvinced about Jimmy. If there are any issues, report back to me immediately. If you get a shot at Jimmy you take it. In this business, it only takes a second and you're dead.' He gestured along the corridor. 'OK, let's go meet our team leaders.'

In the canteen, three spooks – two men and a woman – stood with Two Moons, Gaz, Tug and

Gerald. All three were dressed immaculately in dark suits and had the same grim expression.

'This MI6 lot sure dress up nicely,' said Mitch quietly.

'You should see our CIA people,' whispered back Benny. 'They are fashion personified. Always clean well-cut outfits.'

'There must be good money in spying,' said Mitch, grinning.

'Either that, or they know some really good tailors,' said Benny.

'Let me introduce you to your team leaders,' announced Gerald. 'This is Miranda Jackson. She's one of our most experienced operatives in the field.'

The woman nodded politely. No smile.

'She will be with you, Colonel Nelson, and . . .'

'And Tug,' said Nelson. 'Captain Tait, to give him his full title.' Before Gerald could continue, Nelson added: 'Lieutenant Jaurez will be doubled with Trooper Graham, and Sergeant Two Moons and Trooper Mitchell will work as a team.'

Gerald nodded. 'Andrew Barnes will be with Jaurez and Graham, and John Sparks with Two Moons and Mitchell,' he told them.

From the expressions on the faces of the four MI6 operatives, it didn't look as if they were interested in chit-chat.

'So,' said Sparks walking over. 'You are familiar with the target, James Deacon.'

'Not me,' Mitch corrected him. 'Two Moons and the others are, but I joined Delta Unit after Deacon left.'

Sparks nodded, but so dismissively it was as if he hadn't even heard what Mitch said. It was obvious to Mitch the MI6 agent had something to say to them. Sparks looked around to make sure he couldn't be overheard, then he dropped his voice and snapped at them, 'Right, listen to me. I'm the one in charge. Got that? I know what you SAS types are like. Going off on your own, taking matters into your own hands. Well while you're with me, you do what I say. Understood?'

Mitch looked at Sparks for a moment, then said in disgust: 'That's it? That's the pep-talk?' As Sparks opened his mouth to reply, Mitch reached out and poked him hard in the chest. Keeping his voice low, he went on. 'Listen, we're trained to keep on our toes and survive. We take orders, but we take them from those who've proved to us we can trust them. I don't know you from Adam.

'You can give me orders, and I'll obey them because Colonel Nelson tells me I have to. But if you try playing smart and one of us gets killed because of it, then I'm gonna kill you.' Mitch smiled at Sparks. 'I think you ought to know that.'

Sparks glowered angrily, but before he could respond, the sound of hands clapping made them all look round.

Gerald was standing, smiling at them all. 'Now, I suggest we all return to the briefing room and prepare for the next phase of this operation.'

Sparks got up, threw one last angry glare at Mitch and Two Moons, and headed for the door.

Mitch began walking after him, but Two Moons stopped him.

'Mitch,' said Two Moons quietly. 'I'm no fool. I know why Nelson's put me with you and Gaz with Benny. He thinks we're not up to it.'

'That's not true,' said Mitch.

'Don't try and snow me, Mitch,' said Two Moons. 'He's worried that I won't take Jimmy out if I need to. Well, I got to admit, I don't like the idea. Like I say, Jimmy saved my life, and we were buddies out in the field. That makes for a strong tie. If you want my opinion, I think something happened to Jimmy after he left us and he's gone in the wrong direction. Maybe all he needs is some help and he can get put right.'

'Rehabilitation?' Mitch murmured. 'After six assassinations? If he got caught in some countries he'd be executed.'

'But this ain't one of those countries,' said Two Moons.

Mitch hesitated, then he asked, 'But you're

accepting that Deacon's involved in this?'

'Yeah. I guess I am,' admitted Two Moons awkwardly after a brief silence. 'But, like I say, I hate the idea of killing him.'

'So you want us to try and take him alive?'

'I'd do it for you,' said Two Moons. 'If I thought you needed help.'

'Yes, but I ain't Jimmy Deacon,' said Mitch.

'You're my buddy,' said Two Moons. 'So are all the rest of the unit.'

Mitch thought it over. Then he nodded. 'OK, Two Moons,' he said. 'Let's see what we can do. If we can take him alive, we will.'

Two Moons smiled. 'Thanks, Mitch,' he said.

As Two Moons walked over to the coffee machine, Mitch scowled to himself. He'd just lied to Two Moons. If it came down to it, he was going to kill Jimmy Deacon, and he'd do it without a second's hesitation. But there was no sense in saying that – he needed Two Moons on his side, especially with that idiot Sparks trying to take over.

8

In the next room, a pile of electronic hardware sat on the table. Mitch picked a tiny piece up.

'Mini-headsets,' he muttered.

'Exactly.' Gerald nodded. 'State of the art communication. And to avoid problems with crossed lines, they're set to different frequencies. You, Sergeant Two Moons and Trooper Mitchell, are on the same frequency as your team leader, Mr Sparks. You will be able to communicate freely in a three-way conversation at all times.'

Mitch put on the headset, which would look to any casual observer like a small hands-free mobile phone earpiece.

'In normal circumstances we'd hope to have a trace on the mobile phones these men are using, so we could track them,' Gerald continued. 'However, we haven't yet been able to get hold of the numbers. So, for now, we are going to be tracking them the old-fashioned way: human surveillance, using these devices.

'If you need to change frequencies' – and here Gerald indicated a small dial on the earpiece – 'this will do the job. It can switch over to one of the other teams or bring everyone in – in which case, it has a list of pre-set numbers which will dial back here. To avoid confusion in the field, I would ask that you only change frequencies and talk to the other teams on the orders of your own team leader.'

Yet another thing we have to take Sparks' lead on, thought Mitch grimly.

Also on the table, beside the headsets, was a thin paper file for each team. Mitch and Two Moons picked up theirs and opened it. The photo of the ex-Spatsnatz soldier, Dmitri Pavel, stared out at them.

'Great,' muttered Two Moons. 'We get the ugly

Russian. And Russian is one language I don't speak.'

'No need – I do,' said Sparks, who now stood beside them.

Gaz and Benny had opened their file, and Gaz showed the picture of the French explosives expert to Mitch and Two Moons.

'Looks like I'm going to meet the guy who blew up my door sooner than I expected,' said Gaz.

Andrew Barnes, the agent tasked with being in charge of Gaz and Benny, didn't look amused.

He's going to have trouble with Gaz, thought Mitch.

Nelson and Tug closed their file. 'We'll head to the airport to meet our South African friend,' said Nelson. He turned to Gerald. 'I assume your people are already there, monitoring his flight?'

'Of course. It's on schedule.' Gerald looked at his watch. 'You should make Heathrow with time to spare.'

Nelson nodded, then he and Tug left the room, followed by Miranda Jackson.

'What now, Team Leader?' Mitch asked Sparks.

Sparks ignored the sarcasm in Mitch's voice. 'We follow the Russian and see where he leads us,' he said. He picked up his headset and put it in his ear. 'OK,' he said. 'Let's just test this out. You two stay here.'

Mitch and Two Moons watched Sparks leave the room. They adjusted the earpieces to make sure they felt comfortable. Then Mitch heard Sparks' voice in his ear. 'Red 1 to Red 2 and 3.'

'Receiving you,' said Mitch automatically. Then he asked: 'Which one of us is Red 2, and which is Red 3?'

'Order of rank,' Sparks replied. 'Sergeant Two Moons is Red 2. You're Red 3.'

Mitch looked at Two Moons, who smiled broadly.

'Guess that makes me Second in Command,' he said with a deep chuckle.

Mitch and Two Moons followed Sparks to an underground car park, where a driver was waiting for them. The car was just an ordinary-looking saloon, a dark blue Ford. Nothing that would stand out and draw attention. But Mitch guessed that beneath the bonnet, the engine was supercharged, and beneath the paintwork the sides were armoured.

They got in the car and headed off. As they travelled, Sparks brought them up to date on recent developments.

'We've been keeping Pavel under surveillance since he arrived. Right now he's sitting in a café not far from Euston station. We're going to do this on a rotating watch: I'll pick up Pavel on my own when he leaves the café and follow him for a block or two. Then I'll disappear and Sergeant Two Moons will take over. Then you pick him up, Mitchell. That way he shouldn't spot he's being tailed. Whoever's tailing him will keep in contact with the other two so we're all ready for our change-overs.'

'What happens if he hails a taxi?' asked Mitch.

'We have two taxis of our own on standby.

They'll be near us at all times,' Sparks replied. 'One will follow Pavel if he gets into a vehicle, the other will be ready to take over so he doesn't notice he's being followed.'

'And if he uses public transport?' asked Two Moons.

'If it's a bus, the taxis will be able to follow it. If he gets on a train, we'll make sure we're all somewhere on that train, too, but each in a different carriage,' said Sparks. 'It's a tried and tested method.'

Mitch had to agree. He'd used it many times before when shadowing a suspected terrorist. But with any method of tailing, things could go wrong, and often did.

He checked his personal armoury: the pistol in the holster beneath his left armpit; a knife strapped to each of his lower legs.

Sparks saw this and told him sternly, 'No weapons to be used unless absolutely necessary. These are the streets of London. We don't want innocent bystanders being hurt by wild shooting.'

'If I shoot, it won't be wild,' Mitch assured him.

The car pulled into a kerb near the entrance to Euston station and the team got out.

'You two disappear down that side street until I call you,' Sparks told them.

Mitch and Two Moons nodded, but lingered just long enough to see Sparks head towards a small café. He hailed a man who was standing at a bus stop near the café – they could easily have been two old friends meeting up.

That must be the MI6 watcher on Pavel, thought Mitch.

He looked at Two Moons and nodded. The two soldiers disappeared into the narrow side street, as instructed.

Two minutes later they heard Sparks' lowered voice in their earpieces. 'Red 1: Target leaving café. Heading to Euston station, using the steps in Eversholt Street. Red 2: stay out of sight outside the station in case Deacon is there. He'll recognise you.

Red 3: take position on the main concourse at the station.'

'Copy that, Red 1,' said Mitch.

He crossed the road and walked up the wide stone stairs to the piazza just outside the station, and then walked into the station itself. The concourse was seething with commuters and tourists. Crowds of people stood looking up at the huge display boards, suitcases and bags in their hands, ready to rush for their train. Mitch joined them. He looked up and chose to watch out for the train to Glasgow. On a mission like this, it was important to look as convincing as possible. Mitch didn't know how long he would have to wait. If Pavel was actually going to meet Deacon here, then it could be at any time: ten minutes or half an hour. Mitch didn't think it would be any longer than that – Pavel had such a distinctive, beaten-in face that he would be easily remembered if he was here too long, no matter how big the crowd was. And Deacon wouldn't want to risk that.

The train to Glasgow wasn't due to depart for another forty minutes. That should give Mitch lots of time to hang around on the concourse without arousing suspicion.

He half-turned his head and caught sight of the tall Russian, entering the station. Sparks followed shortly behind him.

Mitch turned his gaze away from the Russian, back to the Departure Board. In his earpiece he heard Sparks say, 'He's not stopping, he's heading out towards the other entrance on the east side. Get in position, Red 2.'

'Copy that,' replied Two Moons.

Suddenly Mitch heard a gurgle through his earpiece. It was an unmistakeable sound – a death rattle.

He turned and saw Sparks tumble to the ground. The tall Russian was striding away, still heading for the side door to the east. Mitch saw him put something into his pocket.

'Red 2 from Red 3,' snapped Mitch. 'Cover's

blown. Red 1's down. Get on to HQ and get someone to him asap. I'm on this guy.' Mitch set off in hot pursuit, dodging the commuters swarming across the concourse.

9

Even as Mitch spoke, a scream came from near Sparks' body.

Someone must have spotted the blood, thought Mitch.

A crowd had gathered quickly, making it hard for Mitch to follow his target. Dropping a shoulder, he barged through a couple of men in suits and sprinted through the eastern exit. Pavel had already disappeared, but across the road he saw Two Moons on the move. His voice came through Mitch's earpiece.

'He's changed direction again, he's heading north. I've got him.'

'OK, but be careful,' Mitch warned his friend. 'He's either carrying a knife or a silenced gun.'

'Trust me, this guy pulls a piece on me, I'm letting him have it,' said Two Moons.

'OK, he's gone through a door leading to a construction site. Ain't no way he'll think I'm just a casual passer-by if I follow him. Especially when there's no noise coming from the site.'

'OK,' said Mitch. 'I'm right behind you.' He broke into a run. He could now see the wooden wall that bordered the construction site, and Two Moons standing by the door.

'I can't risk losing him,' said Two Moons. Mitch saw him pull out his handgun and lean back as he prepared to kick open the door.

'We can't risk losing *you*,' said Mitch urgently. 'For all we know he's waiting for you on the other side of that door.'

'Guess there's only one way to find out,' said Two Moons.

He kicked at the door, smashing it open. The big Sioux stood for a second, waiting for a reaction, and when none came he leapt through the door, ducking down and rolling forwards. Mitch heard the familiar *Phut!* of a silenced gun behind the wall, and then Two Moons yelled in pain.

Mitch jumped into action. He threw himself through the door, pistol at the ready, jerking from side to side to take in the situation.

The Russian was standing abut ten metres away, holding a gun. Two Moons was lying on the ground, his face contorted in agony. Mitch's eyes fixed on the Russian and he shouted the only Russian words he knew, which translated as 'Drop the gun!'

Pavel responded by swinging the gun to take aim at Mitch. But before Pavel could get his pistol centred on his target, Mitch fired off a round. His bullet whipped through Pavel's hand, sending the gun spinning out of his grasp.

The Russian stumbled back, but stayed on his feet. He looked down at his fallen gun and seemed about to grab at it, but Mitch fired again, smashing a bullet into the gun on the ground. Mitch then took aim at the Russian's legs. Take him alive, he thought. He fired, but Pavel moved quickly and threw himself behind a large oil drum.

Mitch swiftly scanned the site. It was clear of workers, but the space was filled with machines and oil drums and small site buildings, piles of concrete blocks, and mounds of piping. The place was a maze; a perfect hiding hole.

'Call backup,' Mitch told Two Moons. 'I'm going after him.'

'He might have another gun,' said Two Moons through gritted teeth. Mitch now saw where he'd been hit, high on the left thigh. Blood was soaking through his clothes.

'I'm OK,' snapped Two Moons, noticing Mitch's worried expression. 'I can tie this up. I've been hit worse before. Go! But watch out for that other gun.'

Mitch nodded and headed deeper into the site. He moved carefully towards the oil drum Pavel had ducked behind. He held his pistol in his hand, ready to fire. Suddenly he threw himself forwards, gun pointed. No one was there.

What weapons would Pavel have? thought Mitch. A knife, probably – Mitch was pretty sure that's what he'd used to kill Sparks. Possibly also a garrotte, a favourite weapon of assassins – a noose of thin, strong wire to drop over the victim's head and slice through the windpipe and the jugular vein.

Mitch stood and listened. The sounds coming from the station and the city outside made it difficult to pick out anything from inside the construction site. He looked around him at the piles of concrete blocks, the machinery, the portable toilets, the shed.

Where would I hide? he asked himself. Not anywhere up high like a crane – too easy to get trapped. Somewhere at ground level, so I could make a quick getaway. Somewhere with shadowy areas for cover.

The portable toilets or the shed. They were close to one another: about ten metres apart. He looked more closely. The door of the shed had a padlock on the outside. Not the shed, then. The toilets.

He moved across the building site, keeping low,

using the machines and piles of blocks and pipes for cover, just in case Pavel had a second gun or a throwing knife.

He made it to the shed without incident. He looked back across at the entrance to the site. Two Moons had dragged himself out of sight, into cover. Mitch wondered how badly he was hurt. If the bullet had broken his leg, he would be out of the game for a very long time. Even if the bone wasn't broken, there was the danger of severe blood loss. By rights he should be treating Two Moons, making sure he stayed alive. But he trusted his team mate. If he said he was OK, then he was.

Mitch looked over at the two portable toilets. The doors of both were shut. Pavel could be inside one, or behind them, or even hiding beneath them. Mitch couldn't use the target's tracks to help him - the ground was a mess of builders' footprints and ruts from the builders and their machines.

Aiming his pistol steadily at the toilets, Mitch inched forwards from the cover of the shed. As he did so, he felt movement behind him. He went to dive to one side, but he was too late. The pistol was knocked out of his hand, and he felt a wire noose slip over his head. Instinctively, he brought his left arm up, palming the garrotte away from his exposed neck. The thin wire cut deep into his hand as he deflected the weapon but the soldier ignored the searing pain. He jerked his right arm back at where he guessed Pavel to be and felt his elbow hit something. His attacker grunted and Mitch twisted and turned to face the man. Pavel was close to him, hanging on grimly to the end of the wire garrotte with both hands. Mitch jerked forwards dragging Pavel with him. He had to break the Russian's grip on the garrotte. In just a few seconds more the wire would slice through his hand to the bone.

Mitch kicked out and felt his heel hit Pavel's shin. The Russian cried out in pain, his leg buckling and his grip loosening on the garrotte.

Taking his chance, Mitch tore his hand from the razor-sharp wire and hurled himself at the big

Russian. Seizing his opponent's wrist, Mitch pulled with all his strength, throwing Pavel forwards over his shoulder. The Russian crashed to the ground where he lay still. His eyes were wide open in a dead stare, a huge metal spike poking up out of his chest. Pavel wasn't going to be fighting back.

When Mitch had flipped him over he'd thudded down on to a piece of contractor's equipment, and the spike had gone straight through him, killing him instantly.

'You OK?'

It was Two Moons. He'd dragged himself across the building site, pistol in hand.

'Are you mad?' demanded Mitch. 'You could have opened up that wound. You might have died from loss of blood!'

'I tried to get near enough to shoot him,' said Two Moons. 'From where I was I couldn't get a proper sight on him, especially when the two of you started jerking around all over the place.'

'He was trying to strangle me,' protested Mitch.

'Excuses, excuses.' Two Moons grinned. Then he gave a groan of pain.

'Bad?' asked Mitch.

Two Moons nodded. 'Yup,' he said.

Just then they heard sirens approaching, and the sounds of vehicles screeching to a halt in the street outside.

'Sounds like the cavalry's here,' said Mitch.

10

Back once again at MI6 HQ. With its metal table and chairs, and dark blank walls on three sides, Mitch felt like he was in an interrogation room. Actually, thought Mitch, this *is* an interrogation room. The fourth wall was a window made of black glass. Behind it would be an observation area.

Mitch sat at the table across from Gerald. His hands were taped up and bandaged, but the deep cuts from the wire still hurt. Another man stood behind Gerald, and a third guarded the door. All three were stony faced. Mitch could see anger in their eyes, and he understood it: their colleague, John Sparks, was dead.

Mitch would be furious and determined to find the culprit if one of his Delta Unit mates was killed.

'What happened at Euston station?' demanded Gerald. 'Why did Pavel kill Sparks?'

It was the third time Gerald had asked this same question, as if repeating it would make Mitch admit something. It was like *he* was the suspect.

'Like I told you before, I don't know,' said Mitch. 'Following Sparks' instructions, my back was turned to them. We were in radio contact. I heard Sparks go down, realised he was in trouble and turned. I went after the Russian.'

'Leaving Sparks to die,' snapped Gerald.

'My orders were to follow Pavel. I radioed Two Moons to raise the alarm, get help for Sparks. But by that time he must already have been dead. Look, the man we were dealing with was a killer. He knew what he was doing. What was it, a knife to the heart?'

Gerald hesitated, then nodded. 'Yes,' he admitted, before quickly changing tack. 'You were supposed to keep Pavel alive. Why did you kill him?'

'It was an accident,' said Mitch. 'I tried to disarm him while he was trying to kill me. I flipped him over to get him off me, and he landed on that spike. That was it.'

Gerald said nothing at first. He was obviously weighing up the situation. Mitch gestured at the room.

'Am I a suspect?' he demanded.

'In what?' asked Gerald.

'You tell me,' said Mitch. 'You certainly seem to be treating me like one.'

'This is standard procedure,' said Gerald. 'A debriefing. You have them after a mission, too, I understand – especially when things go wrong.'

'What went wrong here is that Pavel spotted Sparks,' said Mitch firmly. 'How, I don't know. Maybe Sparks did something . . .'

'Sparks was an experienced field officer,' interrupted the spy angrily. 'He wouldn't have made a mistake.'

'Meaning you think Two Moons or I did?' Mitch snapped back. 'Let me tell you, this wasn't our mistake. Either Sparks did something that gave the game away, or someone gave Pavel the wink.'

'You're suggesting that someone in MI6 tipped Pavel off?' asked Gerald, his eyes narrowing.

'I'm not suggesting anything,' said Mitch. 'I'm just telling you what happened today. Finding out *why* it happened, that's up to you.'

Suddenly the door crashed open and Nelson stood framed in the entrance. Immediately, the man nearest the door pulled out his gun, but Gerald snapped a command and the man put the gun away.

'You're interrupting a debriefing, Colonel,' said Gerald coldly.

Nelson looked angry. 'You've pulled me and my men off the case,' he demanded. 'Why?'

Gerald looked at Nelson, then shrugged. 'Because of what happened,' he said. 'Sparks and Pavel dead, Sergeant Two Moons in hospital.'

'That wasn't down to us!' barked Nelson.

'I don't know that,' said Gerald. 'An operation went wrong. The only people outside of MI6 involved in the operation were your men. Until we've established the facts, Delta Unit are off this case.'

Nelson glared at Gerald. 'You people don't know Deacon like we do,' he said.

'That's one of the things that worries me,' responded Gerald.

Nelson locked eyes with him. Finally, he said: 'I'm taking my man with me.'

'He's free to go.' Gerald shrugged.

Mitch got up and joined Nelson at the door, then followed the colonel out of the room.

As Mitch and Nelson walked away from MI6 HQ, Mitch asked, 'How's Two Moons?'

'He's in surgery,' said Nelson. 'Luckily for him there are no bones broken, and the bullet didn't hit the artery. The damage is mainly to the thigh muscles.'

Mitch nodded. Two Moons would be out of action for a while, but that was all. It sounded like it was nothing serious.

'When can we see him?' he asked.

'Tomorrow,' said Nelson. 'Providing the doctors agree.'

'So, we're off the case?' Mitch asked.

'Like hell we are!' snapped Nelson. 'I'm gonna speak to some people in Washington. No one kicks me off a mission!'

Mitch climbed the stairs to his second-floor flat, still going over in his head what had gone wrong. He pulled out his key and was just about to unlock his door, when he felt something sting his neck. An insect – a wasp?

Suddenly everything switched off: his brain, his body; and he crashed to the floor.

11

When Mitch came round he was slouched on one of the wooden chairs in his living room. Plastic cables tied his ankles to the legs of the chair. His wrists were bound together behind the chair, fixed to the wooden strut at the back. Thick tape had been stuck across his mouth.

He looked up, and found himself staring into the smiling face of Jimmy Deacon.

'Welcome back,' grinned Deacon. He held up a small object. 'Tranquiliser dart. Very effective. You can knock out a horse with one of these.'

Deacon turned his attention to Mitch's living room table, where he was tinkering with something. Mitch couldn't see what it was because it was hidden by Deacon's body.

'So, you're Paul Mitchell,' said Deacon chattily. 'The new guy with the unit. How's that going for you?' Then he grinned again. 'Of course, you can't talk. But I'll take it that you're getting along with them well. They're a good bunch of guys.'

Deacon moved away from the table, pulled a chair near to Mitch and sat down on it, his face close to Mitch's. The smile had gone. 'You killed my operative,' he said. 'Poor old Dmitri. I thought he was good. Obviously I was wrong.' The smile was back. 'But enough of this small talk. Let's get down to the real business of why I'm here.'

He's mad, thought Mitch. Seriously, dangerously mad. He could see it in Deacon's eyes. Everyone in Special Forces possessed a certain ruthlessness – it was how they survived. But Deacon was clearly beyond that. Mitch wondered what had happened to him after he'd left the unit that had driven him to this state. Torture? That often pushed people over the edge.

Deacon gestured towards the table. Mitch

looked and now he saw the wires and explosives and a timer.

'That's right – a bomb, Mitch,' said Deacon, still smiling. 'But this is a very different beast to the little squib I left stuck in Gaz's door. This is a big one. When this baby goes off, not only will it take you out, it'll blow out the apartments upstairs and below.'

His smile became a sneer. 'I guess you're wondering, why you? Well, I'll tell you, Mitch. If I did this to any of the others – my old comrades – they wouldn't forgive that. But you, you're the new guy. They know that you and I don't have a connection. So they'll take it for what it is: a warning to stay out of my way.'

Deacon got up and walked over to the bomb, studying it. Then he turned back to Mitch. 'You may also be wondering why I'm going to all this bother. Why I don't just shoot you dead?' He shook his head. 'It wouldn't have the same effect, Mitch. We know what these spooks are like; they're not to be trusted. They come in and find you dead, they're likely to cook up some story to show that it wasn't me who did it – that it was someone who held a grudge against you. Someone with no connection to this case. Anything to make sure the rest of the Unit will still come after me.

'But this way, this bomb, the guys will know it was me, and that I'm sending them a serious message.'

Mitch growled, his frustration growing at not being able to speak. Deacon saw the anger in his face. 'You look like you've got something to say, Mitch. I'll take the tape off for you to say a few words.' He produced a deadly looking knife. 'But you try to yell out and I'll cut your throat. It won't affect the end result; when the bomb goes off you'll still be dead. But it's a messy way to go.'

Deacon walked over to Mitch, took one end of the tape in his hand and pulled. There was a sharp pain as the tape tore the skin around his mouth.

'So, what do you want to say, Mitch?'

'Killing me won't stop Two Moons and Gaz and the rest,' said Mitch. 'They're my buddies. It'll just make them come after you harder.'

'The old Band of Brothers,' said Deacon. He shrugged. 'Maybe. But maybe not. We'll just have to see, won't we.' He looked at his watch, and then at the timer on the bomb. 'Anyway, we haven't got time to continue this conversation. According to my timer, you've only got about twelve minutes left to live. So, I'll say goodbye.'

With that, Deacon cut off another piece of tape and stuck it across Mitch's mouth. 'Oh, by the way,' he added. 'Don't bother trying to get to those knives of yours to cut yourself free – the ones you keep strapped to your legs.' He chuckled. 'They're not there any more.'

With that, Deacon slipped his own knife into one of his pockets, and headed for the door.

12

As soon as Mitch heard the door shut behind Deacon, he began rocking the chair backwards and forwards, working it one leg at a time towards the table and the bomb. He could see the digital display on the timer as it counted down: 11.48; 11.47; 11.46 . . .

He made it to the table. There was an empty glass near the edge. Careful not to nudge the table too hard and trigger the detonator, Mitch managed to lower his head enough so that his forehead touched the glass. He jerked his head to one side and the glass wobbled, then fell. It rolled along the table top, then dropped off the edge and landed on the carpet.

He looked at the timer. 10.57; 10.56 . . .

Mitch moved the chair so that the fallen glass

was by his feet. He rocked back, then forward, and pounded his boots on the glass, smashing it. He tipped the chair sideways, wincing from the impact as his body hit the floor.

He wriggled his way along the carpet until he was beside the broken glass. Unable to turn his head, he felt with his fingers and found the biggest chunk of glass. Pointing the glass upwards he began to saw at the plastic tie that bound his wrists together. The glass slipped and sliced into his skin, re-opening the wounds on his palms. The blood made the glass slippery and difficult to hold, but Mitch gritted his teeth and continued sawing, flexing his wrists to put pressure on the plastic. The glass sliced his wrists again and again. More blood. Mitch bit his lip against the pain and kept going, aware of the minutes and seconds counting down.

Finally the plastic popped and Mitch could pull his hands apart. He hauled himself up and looked at the timer. 7.35. 7.34.

Mitch tore the tape from his mouth, pulled out

his mobile phone and hit Gaz's number.

'Hi, Mitch,' said Gaz cheerfully. 'What's up?'

'There's a bomb in my flat,' said Mitch. 'Deacon put it here. It goes off in seven minutes.'

'Then get the hell out of there!' snapped Gaz.

'I can't,' said Mitch. 'It's a big one. It'll blow up all the flats around me, so I'm going to try and defuse it. Get on to the emergency services and get the area around my flat cleared. Everyone out to safety.'

'Mitch . . .' began Gaz.

'I ain't got time, Gaz,' said Mitch. 'I've got a bomb to disarm.'

Mitch hung up and turned his attention to the bomb. The timer showed 6.43; 6.42. Just over six minutes to work out how the bomb was rigged, and shut it off.

He looked at the cuts in his wrists, still pumping blood.

I need to strap up the wounds, he thought, staunch the flow of blood. But there's no time. Right now, the main thing is to disarm the bomb.

It looked a simple rig: plastic explosives wrapped round a detonator, and wires attached to the detonator from the timing mechanism. It should be easy. Cut the wires and the bomb stops. But Deacon wasn't a fool – he'd shown how tricky he could be. It was quite possible he'd booby-trapped the bomb. He could have set the timer so that if the wires were cut, it automatically defaulted to zero and triggered the explosion.

Mitch examined the wires. There were four going from the timer to the detonator: blue, brown, yellow, green. Why four? It only took two to make a connection. The other two could be a trick. Maybe one was a dummy lead.

Mitch threw another glance at the count-down display:

5.01; 5.00; 4.59 . . .

He forced himself to think logically: two of the wires are real. The other two are fake. But which is which?

4.41; 4.40; 4.39 . . .

Mitch searched the timer for screw heads. There were none. OK, so it was a clip-together job. That was good; if he'd needed a screwdriver he'd have had problems. He grabbed a shard of broken glass. Blood spurted out from his wrists with the movement. He pushed the tip of the glass into the thin crack in the bomb's plastic casing and pushed, gently so as not to disturb the timer, but with enough pressure to separate one end of the outer casing. He wiggled the glass, working it along the widening crack, until he had a space big enough to get his fingertips in.

He pulled at the plastic and it came apart. At the back of the timer mechanism he could see the ends of the four wires. He flicked the display over to check how much time he had left.

2.15; 2.14; 2.13 . . .

He took a deep breath to calm himself. You've still got two minutes, he told himself.

Four wires: blue, brown, yellow, green. He followed each along with his fingers. The yellow wire disappeared as soon as it ran into the casing

– it wasn't attached to the actual timer mechanism. So it was a dummy. It could be ignored. That left three: blue, brown or green.

He lifted the digital display so he could see the time again:

1.26; 1.25; 1.24 . . .

He remembered the wiring diagrams from his basic bomb training. Brown live, blue neutral. Green was for earth. But a bomb didn't have an earth. So why had Deacon put in a green wire as well? To fool him, or anyone else who tried to defuse it? Or had he replaced the brown or blue with a green wire? A wire was a wire. The coloured plastic was just wrapped round it for safety identification.

23; 22; 21 . . . Twenty seconds to go. 19;18 . . .

He held the piece of broken glass in his hand. Blue or brown should do it. Unless the green was a blue or a brown in disguise.

The clock now showed 7; 6; 5 . . .

Mitch sawed at the brown wire. If he was wrong . . .

He kept sawing with the piece of glass; but the edge had lost its sharpness.

Damn! thought Mitch. I need a knife or wire cutters. But right now this is all I've got. Three seconds. Two seconds. One . . .

The copper wire separated as the piece of glass cut through it.

Then came the explosion.

13

It didn't take long for Mitch to realise it wasn't a real explosion – just the door of his flat being smashed off its hinges. He looked towards the opening. Nelson and Tug were standing there, automatic rifles in their hands. Tug rushed over to the bomb.

'It's OK,' croaked Mitch. 'It's dead.' His throat felt so dry he could hardly speak.

'We were the nearest,' explained Nelson. 'We came as soon as we could.'

'I told Gaz to make sure everyone stayed away,' said Mitch. 'I just wanted the area cleared.'

'Yeah, Gaz told us,' said Nelson.

He bent down and examined the bomb. 'Jimmy up to his old tricks, eh,' he said.

'Yeah,' said Mitch sourly. 'Your old buddy has a wacky sense of humour.'

Gaz and Benny arrived about ten minutes later. By then Tug had sewn up the gashes in Mitch's wrists, and Nelson had dismantled the detonator from the plastic explosives.

'That sure is one big banger,' he commented.

Gaz joined Nelson, examining the bomb. He nodded. 'If that had gone off, it would have taken out most of this side of the building.'

'That's what your friend Jimmy told me,' said Mitch.

Gaz grunted. 'He's no friend of mine, pal. At the beginning, I was prepared to give him the benefit of the doubt, but not after this.'

'It's a pity we're off the case,' murmured Tug. 'If you ask me, this attack on Mitch calls for payback.'

'We ain't off the case yet,' growled Nelson. 'More than ever, this one's ours!'

*

A few hours later Mitch was resting in his flat when he got the call from Nelson.

'Washington came through for us,' he told Mitch. 'They agree that we're the ones most likely to stop Deacon. That's why we were brought in in the first place.'

'I can't believe that Deacon thought that killing me would stop the rest of you,' said Mitch. 'He must know how we soldiers feel about our comrades.'

There was a short silence, then Nelson said, 'If you ask me, it's just goes to show he's really lost it. He's mad, and he's very dangerous. That's why we've got to stop him.'

'Have you spoken to MI6?' asked Mitch.

'Nope. All I know is that Gerald's bosses in Whitehall have had a word with him. He's agreed to us coming back in on this one.'

Mitch grinned. 'He's not going to be a happy bunny,' he said.

'That's his problem,' said Nelson. 'But his real

problem is stopping Deacon, and he knows it. So, we meet up at 10 a.m. at MI6 HQ.'

'I'll be there,' said Mitch.

14

Mitch walked into the small ward in the military hospital. All the way to the hospital he had been on the alert, keeping an eye out for Deacon in case he struck again. Two Moons was lying on his bed, earphones on, nodding in time to some music. He took the earphones off as he saw his friend. Mitch walked over and sat down on the chair beside the bed. He produced a small bunch of grapes, which he put on the bedside table.

'What are they?' asked Two Moons, regarding them suspiciously.

'It's sort of a tradition to bring grapes when visiting a patient in hospital,' replied Mitch, smiling.

'Fruit!' snorted Two Moons. 'I don't like fruit. I like candy. I got shot in the leg – I deserve candy.'

'What can I say? Fruit is better for you,' said Mitch. 'Anyway, I like grapes.' And he picked one off the bunch and popped it in his mouth.

Two Moons looked at Mitch. 'Let me get this straight,' he said. 'You brought me a bunch of grapes so you can eat them?'

Mitch popped another grape into his mouth and nodded. 'Yep,' he said. 'That's part of the tradition. You bring the grapes and then eat them yourself.'

Two Moons thought this over, and shrugged.

'You English are crazy,' he said finally. He noticed the bandages around Mitch's wrists. 'The colonel told me what happened. Sounds like Jimmy stitched you up real bad.'

'It could have been worse,' said Mitch. 'The bomb might have gone off – in which case I wouldn't be sitting here eating these grapes.'

'No, and I'd be getting a visit from one of the others,' said Two Moons, smiling. 'Like Gaz, for example. He likes candy.' Two Moons fell silent.

Finally, he said in a serious tone, 'Jimmy really tried to kill you?'

'Yep,' Mitch replied.

'Son of a bitch!' muttered Two Moons.

'Look at it from the positive side,' said Mitch. 'He didn't try to kill you. He's your friend.'

'Not any more he ain't,' grunted Two Moons. 'Next time I see him, he's gonna get it. No holding back.'

'That's what Gaz said, too,' Mitch told him. 'Glad to know we're still on the same side, Two Moons.'

Two Moons looked uncomfortable for a second, then he nodded. 'It ain't easy to admit someone you thought was your friend is really your enemy,' he said.

Mitch sighed. 'I know. It's happened to me before. Shame we have to learn this kind of thing the hard way.'

'Trust only each other,' said Two Moons.

'Absolutely,' agreed Mitch. He gestured towards Two Moons' leg. 'So, what do the doctors say?'

'They've sewn me up nicely. They reckon I'll be

out of here the day after tomorrow.' He grinned. 'But that's just their opinion. Me, I reckon I'll be walking out of here today.'

Mitch frowned. 'I think, for once, you ought to listen to what they say. Another day or so isn't gonna make a lot of difference.'

Two Moons shook his head. 'This conference thing is only a couple of days away. I want to be there for the action.'

'Not if you're still only working on one leg,' said Mitch. 'Me and the rest of the boys will be worried about you the whole time, which could mean we take our eyes off the ball when Deacon turns up with his gang of assassins.'

Two Moons scowled. 'That's what the colonel told me,' he said. 'And Benny, when he came to see me. You guys been talking behind my back?'

'Nope,' said Mitch. 'It's just logical. You stay and rest it another day, maybe you'll be able to get in on the action.'

Two Moons' scowl deepened. Then he sighed.

'I guess you're right. Only I don't like to think of you guys blundering around out there without me to look after you. Getting yourselves blown up, and stuff.'

'And getting shot,' grinned Mitch.

'So,' asked Two Moons, 'what's next?'

'We've been summoned to a meeting at Spook Central,' said Mitch. 'I guess that, after what happened with Sparks and the Russian, they're having to come up with a whole new plan.'

In the briefing room at MI6 HQ, there was a new air of determination about the men of Delta Unit and the MI6 agents. Any reservations Gerald may have held about the team seemed to have gone.

The fact is, thought Mitch, Two Moons has been shot and is in hospital; I've nearly been blown up by Deacon; one of the spooks has been murdered, and one of the assassins, Dmitri Pavel, is dead. The stakes have been raised, and everyone knows it.

'Pavel may be dead, but Deacon, Smitt and

Lavall are still out there,' said Gerald.

'And under surveillance?' asked Tug.

'Smitt and Lavall are, yes. Despite what happened to Pavel, they don't seem to have been startled into taking cover.'

'Maybe Deacon hasn't told them Pavel's dead,' murmured Benny.

'And maybe he won't,' added Nelson.

'But he must know we're watching them,' said Mitch.

'Perhaps he's assuming that when the time is right, they'll give us the slip,' said Gerald.

Nelson shook his head. 'He wouldn't take that much of a chance,' he said. 'Deacon knows us. He knows what we're like. Once we're on someone's tail we'll hang right on there.'

'Maybe Lavall and Smitt are just decoys?' suggested Mitch. 'We're kept busy watching them instead of looking for Deacon.'

'Maybe,' agreed Benny. 'But we do know there's a connection.' Benny gestured at Mitch.

'Remember, Mitch, Deacon said to you "You killed my operative".'

'True.' Mitch nodded.

'At the moment, these two assassins are the only leads we've got on Deacon,' said Gerald. 'So what I'd like to do is keep them under surveillance. Sooner or later they'll lead us to him.'

'Hopefully sooner, rather than later,' said Nelson. 'The conference begins in just a couple of days.'

'Have your IT people been able to get a fix on their mobile phones yet?' asked Benny.

Gerald shook his head. 'Not yet, unfortunately,' he admitted.

'OK, so we stick to the old-fashioned way,' said Nelson. He looked at the file on the two men again. 'Lavall is staying at the Manxman Hotel on the Strand, and Smitt is in a bed and breakfast place near Victoria station. I suggest this time Mitch and Benny trail Lavall, and Tug and Gaz look after Smitt. I'll stay in reserve, so either team can call me in as backup.'

Gerald shot him a hard look. 'You're excluding my personnel,' he said, tight-lipped.

'I'm sorry,' said Nelson. 'I got the impression you didn't want to work with us so closely any more.'

Gerald was stony-faced. 'This is still an MI6 operation,' he replied curtly. 'However, in light of what happened to John Sparks, perhaps it might be better to keep our teams separate.'

'What happened to Sparks wasn't our fault,' said Mitch.

'I'm not saying it was,' said Gerald. 'I'm just saying it might be better if our people followed you at a distance. We'll keep in contact by the same communications system.'

'So, you watch us watching them?' asked Benny, with a wry smile.

'It does seem logical,' said Gerald. 'That way, if there are any slips, our people can move in unseen and continue the surveillance.'

'If we get killed you mean,' said Gaz with a grim smile.

'No one else is getting killed,' grunted Nelson. 'Not on my watch.'

'Then I suggest we continue the operation,' said Gerald. 'The sooner Lavall and Smitt can lead us to Deacon, the better.'

15

Mitch and Benny were in the lobby of the Manxman Hotel. They had been assured by the MI6 agents watching Pierre Lavall that he was still in his room on the fifth floor.

'Unless he got out the window,' suggested Mitch.

Benny grinned. 'His room overlooks the Strand,' he said. 'If he tried climbing six floors down the face of the building to the street he'd already be on YouTube.' Benny gave a short sigh. 'I know it was a pretty horrendous experience for you, Deacon nearly killing you with that bomb, Mitch, but in a way, it's a good thing it happened. The rest of the unit never really believed me about Deacon. Now, after that, they have to.'

'I'm glad to be of service,' said Mitch with a wry smile.

Just then Tug's voice came over in their earpieces. 'Target Two's on the move,' he said. 'Heading for Victoria station.'

'Copy that,' said Benny. 'No-show from our target so far.'

'Scrap that,' said Mitch sharply. He'd just seen Lavall step out of the lift and head for the reception desk.

Mitch walked across the lobby and out of the door on to the Strand, ready to pick up Lavall as he left the hotel. Benny stayed behind, in case Lavall left by another exit. But the Frenchman handed in his key at reception, and walked out into the busy street.

Mitch let Lavall head off for a few yards before starting to trail him. He was heading west towards Trafalgar Square. Would he stay on foot or take transport? If so, which would he choose: bus, underground or taxi?

Lavall didn't seem to be in any hurry, nor did he appear at all worried that he might be followed. He just kept walking casually along the Strand. Mitch followed at a distance. He was wearing his headset clipped over his ear, just like any other hands-free mobile phone.

He knew that Benny was somewhere close by; possibly on the other side of the road, or in one of the taxis MI6 had provided, staying back and keeping watch, ready to change over.

In his earpiece he received an update from Tug: 'Target Two entering Victoria station. Heading for the underground.'

Mitch was glad the communication system they were using worked underground. Modern coms technology meant you could be in touch with anyone almost anywhere: from outer space to deep below ground level.

Lavall kept walking until he reached Charing Cross station. There, he stopped to buy a newspaper from a stall.

Gives him the chance to take a look around and see if there's anything suspicious or anyone on his tail, thought Mitch.

But he had kept enough distance to avoid being spotted.

Which way now, wondered Mitch? Overground train? Or will he keep walking?

Lavall headed towards the entrance to the underground.

'Here we go,' murmured Mitch into his mouthpiece. 'Target One going underground.'

'Got you,' came Benny's voice.

'Target Two is heading towards the Victoria line northbound,' Mitch heard Tug say.

Mitch wondered if Lavall would also head north. Were the two planning to meet up? If so, the odds were that they'd be meeting Deacon. At the thought of Deacon, Mitch felt a shiver of anger run through him; directed both at Deacon and himself. He'd been careless. He'd let his guard down and allowed himself to be caught. Well that wouldn't be happening again. Next time they came face to face, Deacon wouldn't be walking away.

Still some way behind, Mitch followed Lavall down the stairs to the underground station. He checked the direction they were heading and radioed it back to Benny and the others: 'Bakerloo line southbound.'

Lavall was heading in the opposite direction to Smitt. So maybe there was no meeting with Deacon after all. Maybe the two targets had a different agenda today.

Reaching the southbound platform, Mitch glanced up at the electronic display. The next train would be arriving in one minute. The one after that would come four minutes later. Would Lavall wait and see who else stayed behind on the platform, just to make sure he wasn't being followed? It was what Mitch would do. As both trains had the same final destination, everyone on the platform should get on the first one, unless they had another motive for being there.

The crackle of the railway lines told Mitch the train was coming. Lavall moved forwards to the yellow line at the edge of the platform. Mitch, a few yards further down, did the same. The train slid into the station and stopped, and the doors opened. Mitch stood to let the people get off, and then got on the train. Lavall went to move forwards on to the train, then stopped and stepped back, staying on the platform.

The doors of the train slid shut, and the train moved off.

16

'Target One remained on the platform,' Mitch said into his mouthpiece. He was on the train, leaving the station.

'I thought he might,' said Benny. 'I'm staying at the bottom of the escalator in case he heads back up. I'll keep in touch.'

The next station was Embankment, only a few seconds further on. Mitch got off the train, left the platform and waited in the area by the escalators, out of sight of the platform and the incoming trains. He didn't have to wait long. He heard Benny's voice in his earpiece say: 'Target One on train. I'm in the next carriage.'

'If he doesn't get off at Embankment, I'll grab the train after this,' said Mitch. 'That way I'll stay out of his sight.'

'Copy that,' said Benny.

Mitch waited until he heard the next train pull in.

'Looks like Target One is staying on,' Benny informed him.

'I'll stay here in case he sneaks off at the last minute,' said Mitch.

Lavall stayed on the train and Mitch heard it move off. He then walked on to the platform to wait for the next train. He wondered where the MI6 operatives were. There was no doubt that Gerald would have his own people close behind Delta Unit, out of sight and taking turns to get on and off trains the same way Mitch and Benny were doing.

Mitch caught the next train, which meant he was now just two minutes behind Benny and Lavall.

'End of the line,' announced Benny. 'Elephant and Castle. Target One getting off the train. Heading to Northern line northbound platform.'

'Copy that,' murmured Mitch.

In his ear he heard Tug say, 'Target Two getting off at Euston.'

Euston station, thought Mitch. The place where Sparks had been murdered. Where he and Two Moons had confronted Pavel. Had Deacon chosen somewhere near there for his base?

'He's heading for the escalator,' continued Tug.

Mitch's train pulled in to its final stop at Elephant and Castle. Mitch stepped off and headed towards the northbound Northern line platform. As he walked he took off his black jacket and pulled it inside out. The jacket was reversible; now the lining on the outside was red. A reversible coat was a neat and easy device to avoid being spotted when tailing someone.

'Train arriving,' said Benny. 'I'm getting on it. I'll let you know Target One's movements.'

'Copy that,' confirmed Mitch.

Mitch strolled towards the entrance to the northbound platform, and then stopped in case Lavall appeared and made for the exit after all. He heard the train doors open, and then shut, and the train leave.

'Train on the move. Target One stayed on the platform,' said Benny. 'Looks like he's staying there.'

'Copy that,' said Mitch.

So Lavall was staying put. Maybe he had arranged to meet someone on the platform. Who? Not Smitt, because Smitt was at Euston. Deacon, maybe? Mitch hadn't seen any sign of him, but then, he reminded himself, Deacon was a master of disguise. Maybe he was already here at the station – he could be dressed as a station worker, or anybody going about their daily business.

Mitch heard the sound of another train approaching the northbound platform. He had to take a chance. He walked through the short tunnel on to the platform and spotted Lavall further along. The train was visible now. Mitch decided to let Lavall make the move; see if he got on the train. It was a risk: if Lavall got on and Mitch followed, Lavall might step off again just before the doors closed.

If that happened, Mitch was sunk – he would lose Lavall. And if he rushed off the train, Lavall would spot him as a tail.

There were always the MI6 agents – they'd take over, but Mitch's cover would be blown.

The train doors opened. Lavall got on. Mitch did the same, entering the next carriage. Mitch sat down. If Lavall was going to jump off, Mitch would have to stay on the train anyway, and by sitting down he looked less conspicuous – like a normal guy going about his business. If Lavall had any suspicions, hopefully this would put him off the scent.

The train doors slid shut. Lavall stayed in the carriage.

'Target One on train. I'm in the next carriage,' Mitch reported.

'Copy that,' said Benny. 'I'm at London Bridge station. Getting off now.'

'Target Two on Northern line train, City Branch,' reported Tug.

The same line as us, thought Mitch. He felt a

stirring of excitement. Were the two men going to meet up?

Mitch picked up a discarded newspaper and pretended to read it, while sneaking a glance into the next carriage. Lavall had sat down. The train stopped at Borough station. Lavall stayed where he was. The next stop was London Bridge.

As the train slid into London Bridge station, Mitch spotted Benny on the platform among the crowd. Benny disappeared from sight as the train passed him.

'Stay on the platform,' Mitch advised, 'in case he jumps off.'

'Copy that,' agreed Benny.

Mitch kept his eye on Lavall. The Frenchman stayed in his seat. The doors slid shut and the train moved off.

'I'll follow you on the next train,' said Benny.

'Copy that,' murmured Mitch.

In his ear, he heard Tug say, 'Target Two getting off at Angel.'

'Where's Gaz?' asked Mitch.

'Picking up the train behind this one,' said Tug. 'I'm on Target Two.'

Mitch cast another glance at the tube map. Angel station was just four stops further along the line.

'I've got a feeling our man will get off at the same place,' he said. 'This could be our meeting point.'

'That's how it looks to me, too,' agreed Tug. 'He's heading for the lift. I think we're leaving the station.'

'Copy that,' said Gaz, his voice coming in for the first time. 'I'll be with you in about one minute.'

Mitch kept watch on Lavall in the next carriage as the train stopped at Bank, then Moorgate, then Old Street. As the train approached Angel, Lavall stood up.

'Jackpot,' said Mitch. 'Angel station, confirmed.'

'I'm on the next train,' said Benny. 'I'll be there shortly.'

The train pulled into Angel and Mitch followed Lavall. He kept well back, letting the Frenchman get halfway up the escalator before stepping on himself. Tug was already above ground watching Smitt. Mitch was sure that Smitt and Lavall would meet somewhere near here.

Mitch emerged from the station into the bustling streets. He scanned the area, looking for Lavall. Yes, there he was! The Frenchman was on the other side of the road, heading towards the maze of side streets that backed on to Pentonville Road.

'Come in, Tug,' he said. 'Where are you?'

'Heading towards Chapel Street,' said Tug. 'Target Two in view. You?'

'Same direction, just a few streets behind you.'

'Chapel Street,' said Benny. 'Got that.'

'Me, too,' came in Gaz's voice.

Mitch now slipped off his jacket and reversed it again so the black side was showing. Less noticeable than the red. He saw Tug, standing looking in a shop window. Lavall walked past Tug and continued along Chapel Street. Tug waited until Lavall was out of earshot, then murmured, 'Target One went into Mott & Co warehouse on Chapel Street.'

'Target Two heading towards same warehouse,' added Mitch.

The Mott & Co warehouse was an isolated single-storey building; little more than a corrugated iron shed set on a patch of concrete, surrounded by a chain-link fence.

Mitch stopped and scanned the buildings, as if he was looking for a particular number. He saw Lavall stop outside the metal fence, look around, and then walk through the gateway towards the warehouse. Once Lavall had disappeared from sight, Tug joined Mitch.

'Looks like we've got the location for the meet, Colonel,' Tug said to Nelson through his headset. 'Both targets have gone into the warehouse.'

'Copy that,' said Nelson's voice.

Mitch was aware of movement behind them; someone approaching. He turned and saw Benny and Gaz.

'Looks like we've all ended up at the same place.' Gaz grinned. 'What does that suggest?'

'That our friend Deacon is in there with them,' said Benny grimly.

'Or coming along later,' said Tug.

'Good point,' said Benny. 'OK, let's scatter. We don't want him seeing us. Let's see how this plays out.' Into his mouthpiece he said, 'We're all at the location, Colonel, awaiting orders.'

'Hold it,' came Nelson's voice. 'New orders.'

There was a brief pause, then Gerald's voice cut in and they heard him say: 'Delta Unit, stand down.'

'What?' snapped Benny. 'We've got them in our sights!'

'This is our operation,' snapped Gerald. 'You will stand down, Delta Unit. An armed response team will take over from here.'

17

The four soldiers looked at one another, shocked and outraged. This was *their* operation! *They* had tracked Lavall and Smitt here.

'Colonel . . .' began Tug, but Nelson interrupted him.

'We're being overridden here, guys. Nothing I can do.'

'Colonel, these people don't know what they're walking into,' said Benny. 'We know Deacon. He's tricky. I get the feeling this isn't going to be straightforward. They can't just send in the armed response team. This could be an ambush. Some scam of Deacon's.'

'I've told them that,' said Nelson. 'But this is an Intelligence operation, we're just the foot soldiers. We stay as backup.'

Benny shook his head angrily.

'This ain't Intelligence, Colonel!' he snapped. 'This is lack of intelligence.'

'I think they can hear you,' Mitch pointed out. 'The comms are still on.'

'I don't care!' barked Benny. 'It's madness to crash in there without checking things out.'

Even as he spoke, two black vans appeared. The back doors opened and several armed men encased in black body-armour and armed with automatic rifles leapt out. They headed towards the warehouse, using the surrounding buildings for cover.

'Well, at least they look the part,' commented Gaz. 'I mean, here we are in civilian clothes, with a tenth of their firepower . . .'

'It was still our operation,' muttered Benny. 'These guys don't know Deacon. They don't know what they're going into!'

They heard another vehicle approach from behind them. They turned and saw a car pull up and Gerald and Nelson get out. Nelson looked at his four soldiers with an apologetic shrug.

'Sorry, guys,' he said. 'Being a colonel doesn't carry the same weight here.'

Gerald had gone over to the fence and watched from a distance as some of the response team reached the rusty metal door into the warehouse. Others disappeared round the side of the building, making sure all the exits were covered.

'Anyone come out since Lavall and Smitt went in?'

'No,' said Tug.

'So they're still in there,' muttered Gerald.

'Any sign of Deacon?' asked Nelson.

'Nope,' said Benny.

'So it's likely he was in the building already, waiting for Lavall and Smitt,' said Gerald.

'Or he was somewhere outside, watching and waiting. In which case the sight of your toy soldiers arriving like that will have scared him off,' snorted Benny.

'We know what we're doing,' said Gerald curtly. 'We've been conducting this sort of operation for a long time.' Into his headset, Gerald snapped: 'OK, go. Casualties are acceptable.'

In other words, thought Mitch, kill Deacon and his two fellow assassins. Job done.

Delta Unit watched as the armed response team members nearest them opened the door, then slid silently into the building. They knew the same thing would be happening on the far side of the warehouse. The metal doors swung shut. There was a pause, then they heard the unmistakeable chatter chatter chatter of automatic gun fire, and the next second there was a deafening explosion. The metal doors of the warehouse flew open and fire and black smoke belched out.

'What the . . .!' Gerald shouted, gaping at the scene in front of him.

The five soldiers of Delta Unit already had their weapons drawn and were running towards the warehouse in zig-zag patterns to stop any sniper from getting an easy shot.

Behind them they could hear Gerald shouting into his headset: 'Come in, team! Report! Come in, team!' But the men of Delta Unit knew there wouldn't be any reply. The force of the explosion meant that everyone in that building would have been killed instantly.

18

The emergency services had done their work and gone. The fire was out. The bodies had been removed.

The police had arrived but been sent away by Gerald. Forensics were now examining the smouldering remains of the building. Everyone knew what their findings would be.

'A massive bomb,' said Tug.

Benny sighed. 'We tried to tell you,' he said to Gerald.

The MI6 man said nothing, just turned away, shaken. Mitch looked at the scorched warehouse. 'Deacon intended for Delta Unit to be the ones getting the force of that blast,' he said. 'You guys are the only ones who really know him. You're the only chance there is of stopping him. Once he realised you weren't taking his warnings and backing off, he had to get rid of you.'

'Bit extreme – using his own men as bait,' said Gaz.

'And killing them in the process,' added Tug.

'They were expendable,' said Mitch. 'That's the kind of guy Deacon is now. He's not your pal any more. He's not jolly Jimmy Deacon. He's a ruthless killer.'

'I think Deacon always intended to use Pavel, Lavall and Smitt as decoys – a backup plan in case he couldn't get rid of you as early as he'd hoped,' said Nelson. He turned to Gerald. 'That's why it was so easy for you guys to find them and trail them.'

'A Jimmy Deacon conjuring trick.' Tug nodded. 'He used to do cards tricks, now I recall. This has been a classic case of misdirection. He set those three up for us to follow, while the real team gets on with things without being bothered by us.'

Gerald looked at them, a new expression of horror on his face.

'What?' he asked, his voice hollow. 'Who?'

'Deacon has another squad,' said Tug.

Gerald swallowed. 'But who are they?' he asked. 'We've had no other leads.'

'Ain't that what you're supposed to be the experts in?' asked Benny bitterly. 'Finding out information like that?'

There was an awkward silence, then for the first time since Delta Unit had met him, Gerald's confidence seemed to crack. He hung his head. He looked like a defeated man, thought Mitch.

'Maybe he doesn't have another team?' Gerald said, a note of desperation in his voice. 'Maybe he's working on his own?'

Nelson shook his head. 'Taking out the British prime minister at an event this size, with the place swarming with the Intelligence services and security from twenty countries? This is big. He'll be using backup for this.'

'We have to stop him,' Gerald muttered fiercely. 'We can't let this happen!' He lifted his head and looked at the soldiers, an agonised expression of appeal on his face. 'How do we stop him?' he demanded. 'How do we *find* him?'

'We don't,' said Nelson. 'We let him come to us.'

'We've tried that already,' protested Gerald. 'He got to Trooper Graham – and to Trooper Mitchell.'

'Those were different scenarios,' said Nelson. 'He was in control of them, not us.'

Mitch noticed both Tug and Benny nodding in agreement, and it suddenly struck him: they've been working out a plan. Nelson's next words confirmed it.

'Look, Gerald, so far we've done it by the book. *Your* book. We've followed orders. The end result is that too many of your people are dead, Two Moons is in hospital, Mitch here nearly got killed, and Deacon is still on the loose. All the while, all we've been doing is running around chasing our tails.'

'That is unfair!' protested Gerald. 'There are proper procedures to follow. We're not just some gang of hot-headed soldiers . . .'

'And neither are we,' Nelson cut in firmly. 'We've tried it your way and it hasn't worked. The conference starts the day after tomorrow. Deacon is still out there. If we go on as we have, he'll kill your prime minister for sure. Do you want that to happen?'

'Of course not!' shouted Gerald.

Once again, Nelson didn't give him time to carry on. 'Then hand this operation over to us,' he said. 'To Delta Unit. You brought us in because we know Deacon. You don't. We've got more chance of stopping him than you have. You think you're just dealing with some ordinary assassin. You're not. He's one of us. We trained with him. We fought with him. We know how he thinks, his methods – we know him from the inside.' He pointed at the still smouldering building. 'We advised you against going in like that *because* we know him.'

Gerald stood, his face betraying his inner turmoil. Mitch could tell that every instinct in him, every part of his Intelligence training, told him to say no. But the prime minister's life was at stake, and the spy had already seen what Deacon could do.

'What's your plan?' he asked, finally.

'Like I say, we get Deacon to come to us,' said Nelson. 'I've talked this over with my senior officers, Captain Tait and Lieutenant Jaurez . . .'

Just as I thought, mused Mitch. They've been planning for this.

'You put out a report that the prime minister's had to go into hospital for some minor exploratory procedures just ahead of the conference. But instead, one of us goes in, while you keep the prime minister somewhere safe.'

'What makes you so sure that Deacon will go for the prime minister in hospital? Surely he'd wait until the conference?' argued Gerald.

'No,' said Tug. 'This will seem like the ideal opportunity for Deacon. When's the prime minister going to be easiest to target? At the conference, surrounded by top-level security? Or in a hospital, with just the regular bodyguards on duty?'

Gerald thought it over. 'He'll see through it,' he said. 'He'll know it's a decoy – he's used the same trick himself.'

'We can convince him,' said Benny. 'Deacon knows we've been brought in especially for this because we know him. So we make it public that we're the bodyguards in the hospital.'

'How? Put out a press release?' asked Gerald sarcastically.

'Use the TV,' said Tug. 'Put out the announcement that the prime minister's going into hospital. Show him on the news coming out of Number 10 and getting into a car. I'll be the driver. Mitch and Benny get into the car as bodyguards. The colonel and Gaz get into a second car and we all drive off. Deacon is sure to see it – he'll be keeping an eye on any media surrounding the prime minister.'

'Once we get to the hospital, you lot smuggle the prime minister out and one of us takes his place in the private room,' added Benny.

'But you've got to keep all your troops out of sight,' finished Nelson. 'Make Deacon think it's just us in there, that we're the only line of defence.'

Gerald thought it over. Mitch could tell he was concerned. 'It's very risky,' he said. 'If it doesn't work . . .'

'It's got more chance of working than anything we've tried so far,' said Nelson. 'But *we* have to be in charge. You can have your people as backup, hidden well out of sight . . .'

'Hospital porters, nurses, that sort of thing,' added Tug.

'But *we* call the shots,' said Nelson firmly. 'We give the orders. No one moves without our say.'

Gerald fell silent. Then finally, he nodded. 'Very well,' he said. 'But which one of you will double for the prime minister?'

Nelson grinned. 'I think you can count me out,' he said.

'It has to be me,' said Mitch. 'I'm the nearest to him in build and looks. And, with some good old movie make-up, I'll look right from a distance. From reasonably close-up, even.'

Tug and Benny nodded in agreement. Gaz grinned. 'My pal, the PM,' he chuckled.

'Say Deacon's plan is the same as at the warehouse?' asked Gerald. 'High explosives. He could blow up the hospital.'

'We make sure he can't,' said Benny. 'We use Bomb Disposal to openly scan for explosives. Get them to do the same scans at the conference venue ahead of the summit. When Deacon realises pre-planted explosives are out, he'll be forced to fall back on other strategies.'

'Personal contact,' murmured Tug. 'Gun. Knife.'

'He's likely to be in disguise,' added Gaz. 'A doctor, a hospital orderly, a nurse.'

'We also need to identify and locate the rest of his team,' said Benny. 'Keep an eye on them. Take them out before the attack, if we can. If we can't, at least we'll know who to watch out for.'

'We thought we'd done that,' groaned Gerald.

'We thought Pavel, Lavall and Smitt were the ones.' He paced around, deep in thought. Then he finally said: 'The other team have to be among the bodyguards.'

'At the conference?' asked Benny.

Gerald nodded. 'It's been done before. Body-guards are perfect as political assassins. They've got full security clearance. They're allowed to carry as much weaponry as they like. They'll be the ideal people for Deacon to use.'

Mitch nodded. 'Makes sense to me,' he said.

'That's where I'd be looking as well,' nodded Nelson. 'But which ones?'

'I'll run a security check on every bodyguard attending the conference,' said Gerald determinedly. 'See if there are any who believe they've suffered because of the prime minister's actions. Check out any who are in financial trouble.'

'If there's anything we can do . . .' offered Nelson.

Gerald shook his head.

'This is my department,' he said. 'I'll get my

people on it.' He took out his mobile and began dialling. 'Once we've set that in motion, we can get this hospital business sorted out.'

19

Two hours later Delta Unit met with Gerald in his office at MI6 HQ. Nelson told Gerald he'd chosen the small military hospital where Two Moons was already a patient as the best place to set their trap. He listed his reasons.

'One, we don't have to worry about civilian patients getting injured in any crossfire,' he said. 'Look what Deacon has done so far. He doesn't care who gets killed. We'll do our best to make sure we don't injure anyone else, but we can't speak for Deacon and his team.

'Second, using the military hospital will convince Deacon that we're for real, because it's where we can ensure the best security. And that doubles as the third reason. *We* will be in charge of the situation in there, not some bureaucrat or hospital manager.'

'Makes sense,' said Gerald. Just then his phone rang. 'Yes?' he said. He listened, then looked at Nelson. 'Thank you. Colonel Nelson and Delta Unit are with me at the moment. Prepare the briefing room.' He hung up. 'We think we've got some leads on Deacon's team.'

'Good,' said Nelson. 'Let's see who they've got.'

Delta Unit sat in the briefing room. As before, Gerald was at the laptop with the PowerPoint display. This time there were two silent men, both with bulges in their jackets under their armpits, guarding the door.

'We did intensive background checks on every official member of every party who will be attending the treaty conference,' announced Gerald. 'Six of the bodyguards have been flagged as "possibles".'

'What made their names pop up?' asked Mitch.

Gerald shook his head. 'I'm afraid that's classified information,' he said. 'We've had to work very closely with foreign security on these enquiries. One thing I can tell you for sure: all of them have been associated in some way with Deacon.

'A file has been prepared for each of you containing the photographs you are about to see on screen,' he told them. 'As none of these men have had anything proven against them, it is critical that you ensure these names and pictures are not leaked. We cannot afford an international incident.'

'No problem.' Nelson nodded. 'We're used to keeping secrets, just the same as you are.'

Gerald nodded, then pressed a key on his laptop and a picture of a short-haired, clean-shaven man in a white shirt with dark tie appeared on the screen. He looked like a respectable banker.

'Walter Kornick,' announced Gerald. 'Former US marine, now working for US Government Security. He's here as part of the team protecting the American representative at the conference.'

Kornick's face vanished and was replaced by that of a black man, dressed in the same style as Kornick.

'Edgar Weathers. Like Kornick, he's a former US marine working for US Government Security. He's also here to protect the American representative.'

'Let me guess, Weathers and Kornick were in the same branch of the marines together?' asked Tug.

Gerald nodded.

'Brothers in arms,' murmured Benny.

The picture of Weathers disappeared and an image of a dark-haired man in a military uniform came up on the screen. 'Carlos Dominguez, security with the Argentine delegation,' Gerald told them.

Next up was an unsmiling tough-looking blond man. 'Horst Weissman,' said Gerald. 'Part of the German Ambassador's security team.'

The picture of Weissman now disappeared and in its place they saw a Chinese man wearing the uniform of the Chinese army. 'Pin Chao Lat,' Gerald told them. 'Very well regarded by the Chinese. Excellent military record. Here as one of the bodyguards to the Chinese delegation.' He turned back to the screen. 'And now for our final suspect.'

He clicked for the next picture. As the face appeared on the screen, Mitch let out an involuntary whistle. 'It's Koman,' he said.

Gerald looked at Mitch. 'You know him?' he asked.

'We all know him,' said Nelson. 'Mehmet Koman. We were on an operation recently in Turkey. Koman was our link with Turkish security.'

'He's also a damn good operative,' said Benny. 'You sure he's working with Deacon on this assassination?'

'We did extensive cross-checks working with the Intelligence services of the other countries who are coming to the summit,' Gerald told him. 'Finance, politics, personal tragedies, every last little piece of info. Then we did more cross-checks and carried on digging. These are the ones who fit the profile best.'

'But we don't know for sure,' said Mitch.

'They're the most likely suspects, Mitch,' said Nelson. 'And, remember, we all felt the same doubts about Deacon when this started.'

'True,' agreed Mitch.

'OK, so what's the score with these guys?' Nelson asked Gerald. 'Do we take care of them, or what?'

Gerald shook his head. 'I'm afraid there are political issues to be taken into consideration. We've alerted our counterparts in their own Intelligence services about our concerns. I've been assured that the suspects will be kept under close observation the whole time they are here.'

'So hopefully we've isolated Deacon,' said Tug.

'Unless he puts another team together,' said Gerald.

Nelson shook his head. 'One, he doesn't know we know about his team. Two, even if he did, he'd have no time to put together another outfit.' He looked around at the rest of his unit. 'All we can do is hope the intel's good, and that we get lucky.'

20

Two Moons was sitting in a chair in his hospital room when the rest of Delta Unit walked in. He looked up at them in surprise.

'Hey, guys, don't think I'm not touched by this, but isn't all of you coming to visit me at once slightly overdoing it?' he asked.

'We're not just visiting,' Nelson told him. 'We're having an ops meeting.'

Briefly, Nelson filled Two Moons in on the plan. When he'd finished, Two Moons turned to Mitch with a broad grin.

'And you're gonna be the prime minister?' he chuckled.

Mitch grinned back. 'You're welcome to take on the role, Two Moons,' he said.

Two Moons shook his head. 'You know as well as I do that ain't gonna fly.'

'They're going to use make-up on Mitch,' pointed out Gaz. 'I'm pretty sure a good make-up artist could do a convincing job on you.'

Two Moons looked aghast. 'Make-up?' he said. 'In that case I am *definitely* not doing it!'

'Can we get down to details?' said Nelson. 'The clock's ticking and every second is precious. Let's talk about where the trap is going to be set.'

'The top floor,' suggested Benny. 'It makes it harder for Deacon and his men to get to the target because there are more obstacles. And the top floor isn't overlooked, so we cut down the risk of Mitch getting shot from the window of a building opposite.'

'I agree with that.' Tug nodded. 'Though the roofs of the buildings opposite could be a problem. I checked it as we came in. They're on the same level as the windows of the top floor of this hospital.'

'We'll get Gerald's men to cover the roofs of the surrounding buildings,' said Nelson.

Mitch's mind flashed back to Istanbul, and working with Koman.

'We ought to have someone on the roof here, too,' he said. 'Remember Istanbul? Koman said to me that if he was doing a job he'd use the roof.'

'I'll take the roof,' said Gaz. 'It'll be useful to have a couple of Gerald's people with me. Three of us should be able to handle it.'

'Leave that to me,' said Nelson. 'I'll fix it with him.'

'We also need to make sure the windows of the room where Mitch is gonna be have bullet-proof glass and wire in them,' added Benny.

'Right,' agreed Nelson. 'Two Moons, how you feeling?'

'I'm perfectly fine,' said Two Moons. 'I should have been out of this place days ago. I told Mitch . . .'

'Yeah, yeah,' sighed Mitch. 'We all know you're invincible. But the fact is, if your wound had opened up again . . .'

'It won't,' said Two Moons firmly.

'We use the fact that Two Moons is already in this hospital to our advantage,' said Nelson, cutting their argument off before it could escalate. 'Two Moons, we'll have you moved up to the top floor, in the room right next to Mitch's. That way you're on hand and ready for action if needed.'

'Suits me,' said Two Moons cheerily.

'Mitch, you'll have all the weapons you need stashed within easy reach,' continued Nelson. 'Two Moons, same for you.'

'Body armour under your pyjamas, of course,' murmured Tug.

'Good com headsets,' added Benny. 'Communication at all times.'

Nelson unfolded a plan of the hospital, showing the stairwells and the lifts.

'OK, guesses as to how Deacon and his boys are going to make their attack?'

'Disguised,' said Tug. 'Hospital orderlies, or doctors, or nurses.'

'Which suggests to me they'll be using one of the

big lifts,' put in Gaz. 'Maybe with a bed or a trolley, with their weapons hidden in it.'

'OK, so we disable all the lifts except one,' said Nelson. 'Tug, you and me stay close to the functioning lift on the top floor.

'Benny, you'll be in the landing of the stairwell for the top floor. Me or Tug will be on the other side of the door, ready to join you if the attack comes that way.'

'I suggest we all have gas masks ready,' said Benny. 'Deacon's tricky. Remember, he used a tranquiliser dart to knock Mitch out. He's just as likely to use a disabling gas in the stairwell.'

'Or when he comes out of the lift,' pointed out Mitch. 'If he uses the lift, he could be bringing anything up: flash-bangs, grenades, whatever.'

'Good point,' agreed Tug. 'We need a lift operator to check everyone entering the lift.' He smiled. 'I'll volunteer for that.'

'If one of them's Deacon, he'll recognise you,' pointed out Gaz.

'Deacon will recognise all of us,' said Benny. 'And he knows we're going to be here. This ain't about him recognising us, it's about us recognising him.'

'In other words, we don't hide,' murmured Tug. 'We're in plain sight.'

'Let's get back to the business of the lift,' said Benny, turning to Tug. 'You'll be on your own. Say two of them get in the lift. You won't have much chance.'

'I'll keep an alarm gripped in my hand every time I open the lift door,' replied Tug. 'The sort that only works when you release it.'

'Dead Man's Hand.' Two Moons nodded.

'I prefer to think of it as Unconscious Man's Hand,' chuckled Tug. 'If they attack me, whatever happens, I'll loosen my grip on the alarm and it will go off, and you'll know they're in the lift.'

Nelson frowned. 'I'm not happy with this,' he says. 'You're too important to lose, Tug. Especially that early in the operation. I think I'd prefer to use one of Gerald's men as the lift operator.'

Tug shook his head. 'With respect, Colonel, the reason we were brought in to this in the first place is because we know Jimmy Deacon. If he walks into that lift, I'll know him and I won't hesitate.'

'Tug's right, but how about a compromise,' suggested Benny. 'Make sure that there's always one of Gerald's people, dressed as hospital staff, in the lift with Tug. Fully armed.'

'Good idea,' agreed Nelson. 'I'll buy that. And I know Gerald will. He wants his people to be right at the heart of the action.' He looked around at his men. 'Let's recap: Mitch in the room. Two Moons in the room next door. Gaz on the roof with a couple of Gerald's men. Benny in the stairwell. Tug in the lift. Me on the top floor by the lifts, ready to join Benny if needed. Is that it?'

The others nodded.

'And Gerald's people on the ground floor as a first line of defence and possible backup,' added Benny.

'OK, we have a plan.' Nelson checked his watch. 'So, let's get it moving. I'll get back to Gerald and set things up. Hopefully he'll have organised the media to cover the prime minister coming here this afternoon. And after that, it's up to us.'

21

Phase One of the plan swung into operation within three hours. A press release had already been issued stating that the prime minister was going into hospital for a minor medical procedure; and that he had chosen to go into the military hospital as an expression of solidarity with the troops who were recovering from injuries received while fighting for their country. When Mitch read this, he shook his head in disbelief.

'Politicians!' he said to the others. 'They grab any opportunity to chase votes!'

At 3 p.m. two heavily armoured limousines drew up outside 10 Downing Street and Nelson and Tug entered the building. Like the rest of Delta Unit they were wearing civilian clothes: dark suits, with noticeable bulges near their arms where they wore their guns. Mitch, Benny and Gaz got out of the cars and stood waiting by the entrance to Number 10, making sure the TV cameras caught them. Deacon had to be convinced that this was no trick – that Delta Unit was taking control of the prime minister's personal close protection.

A few moments later Nelson and Tug escorted the prime minister out of Number 10. They paused on the doorstep long enough for him to answer a journalist's question and to reassure the nation that he was in good health and that he would still be attending the terrorist treaty conference when it opened. Then he walked with Nelson and Tug to one of the cars and got in. The other soldiers followed suit, and then the cars set off on the short drive to the military hospital.

There were more TV cameras outside the hospital, awaiting their arrival. Their every move was captured on TV. Deacon would surely be in no doubt that the prime minister had been delivered to the hospital.

Phase One accomplished, the plan entered Phase Two.

Inside the hospital, three of Gerald's people were waiting, all wearing white coats and with ID tags identifying them as doctors. They carried a fourth white coat, similarly tagged with an ID card, which they slipped on to the prime minister once he was safely inside the building. They added a false moustache and a pair of glasses to his face, then the four of them strolled out of the rear entrance of the hospital to the car park where they got into a military ambulance and drove off.

The five soldiers of Delta Unit headed up to the top floor of the hospital. They nodded at Two Moons, now ensconced in an upstairs room, and entered the room designated for Mitch. The curtains of the window had already been pulled.

Two make-up experts were already in the room, dressed as nurses. They gestured to Mitch to sit in a chair by a dressing table, and then they set to work. Thirty minutes later, with the help of hair dye, pads in the sides of his mouth to push his cheeks out, and shadows under his eyes, Mitch bore a passable likeness to the prime minister.

The make-up artists packed up their gear in medical cases, then headed downstairs where they were met by more of Gerald's people and escorted to a secret location until after the conference. MI6 and Delta Unit were taking no chances – loose talk could cost them the operation and their lives.

With just 48 hours to go before the conference began, Delta Unit needed Deacon and his hired assassins to make their move now. The trap was set. Now it needed to be sprung.

22

Mitch sat on the hospital bed and looked across at Nelson, who was hovering near the one operating lift, an automatic rifle cradled in his arms. Mitch knew Two Moons was poised for action in the next room. He had popped in for a brief chat earlier, dressing gown on and with a slight limp from his bullet wound, but he was ready to go, rifle at the ready.

Soldiers feel naked without a weapon of some sort, Mitch reflected.

Mitch's own weapons were to hand. His M80 and his favourite handgun, the H&K23. Like the other soldiers, he had a gas mask within easy reach, just in case Deacon used some sort of chemical weapons in his attack.

The time was dragging now. Trust me to be

willing an assassin to hurry up, he thought.

He considered the chance that Deacon would wait until the prime minister was at the conference. That would be bad news for the unit. They needed to get this dealt with, and soon. This was their only real chance of stopping Deacon.

Every so often Nelson would check on Mitch and Two Moons, and make contact with the rest of the unit via the comms link.

'Gaz?'

'Everything's quiet on the roof,' reported Gaz.

'Tug?'

'No action in the lift so far,' said Tug.

'Benny?'

'All quiet on the stairs.'

The first word of movement from the opposition came at ten o'clock that night. Nelson's voice came through the unit's earpieces. 'Word from Gerald: five of those bodyguards have disappeared from their posts and gone off the radar. They think it's happening.'

So much for keeping them under close surveillance, thought Mitch.

But then, these guys were all special forces. Getting out from under close surveillance is what we're trained to do.

'Makes sense – it's going to be a night attack,' said Two Moons.

'Which five?' asked Benny.

'The two Americans, Kornick and Weathers; Koman, Dominguez and Weissman.'

'So the Chinese guy turned out to be OK,' said Gaz.

'We don't know that for sure,' said Nelson. 'All we do know is those five are on the move.'

'When did anyone last see them?' asked Tug.

'According to MI6, about two hours ago.'

Two hours ago, thought Mitch. They could be anywhere by now. They could be right outside the building at this very moment. He wondered where Deacon was. Deacon was the key. The real danger.

Suddenly a voice came through his earpiece. It

was Nelson, and he sounded angry.

'I've just had an update from Gerald,' he said. 'It turns out that Kornick didn't vanish two hours ago. He's been missing since early this morning. He reported in sick, which is why the Americans didn't pick up on it. It was only when someone went to his hotel room to check on him they found he'd gone.'

A hundred thoughts raced through Mitch's head. Kornick had had all day to set a plan in motion. From before they'd even brought the prime minister to the hospital.

Mitch swung his legs off the bed and began to pace around the room. This was a trap and he was the bait. It was that simple. He was the target.

Gaz's voice came through his earpiece. 'The roof is still secure. Everything OK.'

Let's hope those really *are* Gerald's men with Gaz on the roof, thought Mitch. Deacon could have easily pulled a switch. He went back to the bed and sat down, nerves jangling, but on full alert.

Some sixth sense suddenly made Mitch look up.

There, in the ceiling, directly above his hospital bed, was a dark round spot. No, not a spot. A hole. Something was being pushed through. The barrel of a gun!

23

Mitch rolled and threw himself off the bed, just as a bullet thudded into the spot where he had been lying a split second before. He swung his automatic rifle up at the spot in the ceiling and started firing, letting the bullets tear into the plaster above him as he twisted the gun in a circular motion. He rolled again as he saw the plaster bulge, then something – someone – crashed through the weakened ceiling and was falling downwards, smashing into the bed.

The gunfire had brought Nelson and Two Moons running. They stood in the doorway, rifles ready but stunned at the sight of a body on the bed.

Gaz was calling on the headset: 'What's happening? Someone just shot a burst right through the roof!'

'That was me,' said Mitch. 'It's OK.'

'What do you mean: OK?' demanded Gaz indignantly. 'We could have been killed up here!'

'Stop complaining, the ceiling and joists would have taken most of the impact,' argued Mitch.

'You planning on shooting through the roof any more?' said Gaz.

'Not any time soon,' answered Mitch.

Two Moons aimed his rifle at the hole that had appeared in the ceiling, and Nelson joined Mitch by the bed. The attacker was dead, the telltale exit wounds visible at the back of his head. He was wearing Kevlar body armour, but Kevlar didn't protect the head, neck, arms and legs. Mitch's blind shooting through the ceiling had torn into the man in all those places.

While Mitch kept his gun ready for action, Nelson turned the man over so they could see who it was. Was it Deacon? No. It was Walter Kornick, the CIA agent.

'One down,' murmured Mitch.

Two Moons looked up at the shattered ceiling.

'How the hell did he get in there?' he demanded.

'He must have got up in the ceiling cavity some time before we arrived here,' muttered Nelson. 'He parked himself up there, ready to bore himself a nice little spy-hole.'

'How did he know which room I was going to be in?' demanded Mitch.

Nelson shook his head. 'I don't think he did,' he said. 'He must have waited until you moved in before positioning the spy-hole.'

'But how did he do it without you noticing, Mitch?' asked Two Moons.

Mitch sighed. 'I can't believe I'm going to say this, but I had to go to the toilet this afternoon,' he said. 'I figured with the colonel in the hall, everything was secure. I didn't factor in the ceiling cavity! I guess he used that opportunity to make his move.'

'So why didn't he shoot you earlier? Why now?'

'I think he was intending to get away,' said Nelson. 'That meant waiting till it was dark. Shoot Mitch, then smash his way out through the roof.'

Two Moons shook his head suspiciously. 'I don't like it,' he said. 'There are too many coincidences. If you ask me, someone inside this operation is leaking intel to the opposition.'

'One of Gerald's people?' asked Mitch.

'Well I sure ain't suggestin' it's one of Delta Unit!' snorted Two Moons indignantly.

Nelson turned to Mitch. 'What do you think, Mitch?'

Mitch shook his head. 'No,' he said. 'Don't get me wrong – I don't trust spooks, but in this case, if Deacon really knew what our plan was he wouldn't be here trying to kill me, he'd be going after the real prime minister.'

Two Moons gave a scowl. 'Damn! I should have thought of that!' he grunted.

'What's the situation?' came Benny's voice.

'Kornick tried to shoot Mitch,' Nelson reported. 'He was hiding in the ceiling of Mitch's room. Luckily Mitch shot him first.'

And then the lights went out.

24

It was pitch dark.

'Night vision!' yelled Nelson. The soldiers were already pulling on their goggles.

'He must have blown up the transformer that supplies electricity to the whole area,' said Benny.

'Guys, I've got a problem,' came Tug's voice. 'I was in the lift between the first and second floors when the power went. I'm going to have to get up through the trapdoor in the roof and climb up the cable. Can anyone see if they can get the lift doors on the second floor open for me?'

'You're gonna have to stay there for the moment, Tug,' replied Nelson. 'We got something urgent on our hands.'

'Copy that,' said Tug.

'Why hasn't the emergency generator cut in?' demanded Benny.

'I guess Deacon's dealt with that, too,' said Nelson. 'OK, boys, keep sharp. We don't know which way they're coming from, but with the power gone it has to be the stairs and the roof.'

'Copy that, Colonel,' said Benny. 'I just heard gunfire below.'

'I'm with you,' said Nelson.

Mitch saw Nelson rush through the door to the stairs. The next second rapid gunfire came from the stairwell.

Two Moons appeared from his room to take Nelson's place in the corridor by the doors to the lifts, becoming the last line of defence between the attackers and Mitch's room.

A burst of automatic gunfire from above made Mitch look up.

'They're on the roof!' came Gaz's voice over the gunfire. 'Two of them.'

So, Deacon wasn't using any disguises after all,

thought Mitch. Just a straightforward, full frontal attack. Two on the roof. There had to be two in the stairwell. So where were the others?

The answer came quickly. A figure dropped out of the ceiling and landed right on Two Moons. Mitch watched as Two Moons battled with the assailant. In hand-to-hand combat an automatic rifle was no use. Two Moons had discarded his, and was getting to grips with his attacker, fists and feet striking out as both men tried to get the advantage. There was a flash as a knife blade appeared in the attacker's hand.

Mitch swapped his automatic rifle for his H&K23 pistol and tried to get a clear aim at the man, but it was impossible while he grappled with Two Moons.

Where was the other assassin, Mitch wondered?

He heard the *phut* of a silenced gun and felt a thud in his chest as his body armour took the bullet, the force of it sending him staggering backwards. He recovered his balance and swung his gun towards the corridor. As he did so there was another *phut* and a searing pain in his right hand. His pistol was torn out of it and went clattering to the floor. Clenching his teeth against the pain, Mitch reached down for his fallen pistol, but another shot sent it spinning away from him.

Mitch looked up. A man dressed completely in black had just entered the room, night-vision goggles in place and a pistol in his hand.

'I'm sorry about this, Mitch,' said the man. Mitch couldn't believe it. It was Mehmet Koman! 'I got suspicious when I saw you holding a pistol,' said Koman. 'It struck me that it didn't seem the sort of thing a British prime minister would do.'

'Where's Deacon?' asked Mitch.

'Where's the prime minister?' Koman countered.

Mitch shook his head. 'It doesn't have to be this way, Mehmet,' he said. 'The job's a bust. Give yourself up.'

'And what happens then?' demanded Koman. 'When I get back to Turkey? I'll be killed. Not officially, of course, but we both know how it will happen. An "accident".'

'You'll stand trial here,' said Mitch.

Koman laughed. 'I won't be safe here, Mitch, and you know it,' he said. 'There are powerful and very rich people behind this operation. They won't want us alive and talking.' He hesitated, and then added: 'I have to finish this job.'

'Why?' appealed Mitch.

'Money, of course,' said Koman. 'What else?'

'But why this way?' asked Mitch. 'I was told that Jimmy Deacon was some master of disguise. Yet you're coming in like a parachute battalion.'

'It seems our paymasters want it this way,' said Koman. 'Lots of carnage and explosions so everyone will know what happened, and why. It's a message. Don't mess with these boys.' He shrugged. 'That's the way they want it, that's the way they get it.' He jabbed the pistol at Mitch. 'Now answer the damn question. Where's the prime minister?'

Out of the corner of his eye Mitch saw Two Moons crash to the floor, his assailant on top of him. Gunfire was still coming from the stairwell and the roof above him. No one was coming to save him any time soon.

'Forget it, Mehmet,' said Mitch. 'You're gonna kill me anyway.'

Koman shook his head. 'I always keep my word, Mitch,' he said. 'If I say I'm going to kill the prime minister, I'm going to do it. If I say I'll spare your life if you tell me where he is, I'll do it.'

'No you won't,' said Mitch. 'You're a professional.'

Beneath his night-vision goggles, Mitch saw Koman's mouth curve into a rueful smile.

'Maybe,' he said. 'And right now I'm a professional holding a gun on you, and I might be telling the truth. One thing I *will* promise you, if you don't tell me where the prime minister is when I count to five, I'm pulling this trigger. Because I intend to get out of here alive, but we need to know where our target is.'

Koman pointed the gun firmly at Mitch's head. Mitch tensed, ready to throw himself towards Koman, but he knew he'd have no real chance. The Turk had made sure he was at a safe distance from Mitch.

'I'm getting impatient, Mitch,' said Koman. 'The countdown starts now. Five. Four. Three. Two. One . . .'

BANG!

25

The shot, when it came, exploded in Mitch's night-vision goggles in a blinding flare of white. Mitch threw himself to one side, expecting to feel the pain of the bullet tearing into the side of his head, but nothing happened.

He crashed into the hospital bed and recovered his balance as a second shot rang out. He looked around, towards Koman. The Turk was lying on the ground, writhing in pain. Behind him stood Tug, automatic rifle in his hands.

'Seems I got out of the lift just in time,' said Tug. 'You OK?'

'Apparently so. Thanks.' Mitch nodded.

Two Moons got to his feet next to Tug, looking down at his assailant whom Tug had also dispatched. 'Who's that?' he asked.

'Mehmet Koman,' said Mitch.

In their earpieces they suddenly heard Gaz: 'I'm hit!'

'I'm coming up!' responded Mitch.

'Me too!' called Tug. They ran for the door to the stairs, Mitch snatching up his rifle on the way. As he did so he called to Two Moons, 'Keep your eye on Koman. He's tricky!'

'Don't worry,' said the big Sioux. 'I'll take care of him.'

Inside the stairwell, Nelson and Benny were keeping up a steady stream of fire as they worked their way down the stairs, forcing the attackers back down towards the lower floor and the MI6 backup.

Tug raced up the stairs towards the roof, Mitch close behind him, both of them tearing off their night-vision goggles as they did so. On the roof, with the lights of London giving them sight, the goggles would be more of a hindrance than a help.

They crashed through the doorway on to the roof, both of them rolling as they did so to avoid being hit. They dived behind a low parapet. Tug was the first to regain his position and balance and he swung round, levelling his rifle, taking in the situation. A burst of gunfire smashed into the bricks of the parapet, sending a shower of stones and shattered brick pieces over him. The captain responded immediately, letting off a tracer of bullets in the direction the shots had come.

Mitch saw Gaz lying on the roof, one arm trailing brokenly beside him. A dead MI6 man lay next to him. Gaz was struggling to hold his rifle with his one good arm. Mitch worked his way towards his friend, speaking into his mic: 'Gaz down. Two hostiles still operative. Support needed.'

Mitch used a knife to rip open Gaz's sleeve so he could see the wound. The bullets had torn an ugly hole in the Geordie's upper arm as they exited, after breaking the bone.

'It's not pumping,' Mitch said. 'They didn't hit

an artery, but you're still losing blood. I'm going to have to tie it up.'

'Hurry up!' groaned Gaz. 'We got a battle to win.'

Gaz winced in pain as Mitch placed a large dressing from his field pack over the wound, and then fixed it in place with an adhesive bandage. All the while Two Moons and Tug were firing, and return fire was coming back at them, bullets ricocheting of the stonework beside them.

'Rest it now,' Mitch instructed Gaz. 'Leave it to us.'

With that, Mitch snatched up his own automatic rifle and joined in the firefight. Suddenly he saw that one of the attackers was sliding away, heading for the edge of the roof.

'Cover me!' yelled Mitch. He broke into a run, chasing the man, his rifle pouring bullets. But the attacker dived behind a chimney stack. There was no return fire from him.

He's out of ammo or his gun has jammed, thought Mitch.

Mitch sped towards the chimney stack, zig-zagging as he ran. He was aware of the bullets continuing to fly behind him as Tug engaged the other assailant. Mitch reached the chimney stack and saw the attacker break out of hiding and make a definite run for the edge of the roof. He was obviously planning to jump across the gap between the hospital roof and that of the next building. Mitch aimed low at the running man's legs and pulled the trigger . . . and nothing happened. He was out of ammo too.

There was no time to pull out the empty clip and replace it – by the time he did that the attacker would have vanished.

Mitch dropped his rifle and gave chase. When they'd checked out the hospital and the surrounding area before this operation, the gap between the buildings wasn't just straight across; there was also a drop of about three metres. The attacker reached the edge, jumped and disappeared out of sight. Mitch, hot on his heels, ran faster to make sure he was at speed when he hit the edge. As he reached it he propelled himself with as much force as possible into space. He was aware of the street dizzyingly far below him as he sailed through the air, then he was dropping and the next roof was coming up fast. He just made the edge and rolled forwards, then sprang up.

As he did so he felt a sharp, searing pain in his right ankle. He was sure he'd fractured a bone. He cursed and looked up. The man also looked to be limping badly as he tried to run. He had definitely injured himself in making the jump.

Mitch reached for his pistol, then realised it was still on the floor of the hospital room where Koman had shot it out of his hand. He was unarmed, except for his knife. He wondered what sort of weapons the attacker had on him.

'Halt or I shoot!' yelled Mitch.

It was a bluff, but it was one worth trying. The man stopped limping along and turned towards Mitch.

'Well, well,' he said. 'We meet again, Mitch.'

In the dim light Mitch couldn't see the face clearly. But he recognised the voice. It was Deacon.

26

'Don't make me shoot you!' called Mitch.

'With what?' asked Deacon, his tone mocking. 'If you had a gun you wouldn't even be talking to me. You'd have shot me by now.' He shook his head. 'I think this conversation is over.'

And with that he turned and began to limp away fast. Mitch tried to follow, but his ankle buckled beneath him. 'Damn!' Mitch cursed.

Mitch pulled his knife out, balanced it, and threw it as hard and as accurately as he could, aiming for Deacon's legs. It would be no use hitting the body armour.

Deacon gave a cry of pain and crumpled to the roof. Mitch had struck home. He hopped as fast as he could to where Deacon lay, his ankle sending waves of pain through him with every movement.

Deacon rolled and pulled the knife from his leg, then held it pointed towards Mitch as he reached him.

'Give it up, Deacon,' urged Mitch. 'The rest of your squad is gone. It's over.'

'Not for me,' groaned Deacon through gritted teeth. 'There's always a new identity. I can start again.'

He struggled to get to his knees, holding the knife firmly in Mitch's direction. Mitch hesitated. With his ankle fractured he couldn't run at Deacon. If only he had something he could use as a weapon, *anything*. But the only thing he had was himself.

He hopped painfully nearer, his eyes on the knife. Deacon crawled backwards.

'Look at us, Mitch.' Deacon chuckled painfully. 'We've only got two good legs between us. We're in a bad way.'

'I'm not letting you get away,' said Mitch firmly.

Deacon shook his head. 'You don't have a choice, Mitch,' he said.

Suddenly he threw the knife at Mitch and rolled towards the nearest edge of the roof. The knife flew past Mitch's head as he hurled himself at Deacon, pain searing through him from his ankle. He managed to grab hold of one of Deacon's legs, his fingers clutching at the material. Deacon struggled and kicked out, trying to loosen Mitch's hold. Mitch held on grimly, but Deacon was still able to drag himself ever nearer the edge, pulling Mitch along behind him. Using all his strength, Mitch hauled himself hand over hand up Deacon's leg to his body. Deacon struck out, his fists hitting Mitch on the head and in the face, while at the same time he continued to push with his good leg, right to the very edge of the building.

With a last heave Mitch managed to get a hold on Deacon's neck. Now both men were right on the edge. Mitch saw the street below, and a window ledge about four metres below the edge of the roof. It was impossible to think that Deacon would even try such a drop – but then Mitch realised

Deacon was a truly desperate man. He was fighting for his life.

A sudden punch to his face from Deacon brought tears to Mitch's eyes, temporarily blinding him, but he clung on grimly. He felt a shift and as his eyes cleared he realised they were balanced precariously, their heads right out over the drop of over fifty metres to the street below. Then suddenly, with a jerky movement from Deacon, they rolled off the edge of the roof, into the void!

As they fell, Mitch yelled in agony from the pain in his fractured ankle. He just had time to let go of Deacon with one hand and grab hold of the window ledge. He smashed into the wall below, but his left hand still clutched Deacon's clothing.

The two men dangled, the cars and people in the street far below them looking to Mitch like small toys.

I can't hold him, thought Mitch. He's too heavy.

Deacon's weight felt like it was tearing his arm

out of its socket, especially with the way he was struggling.

'Mitchell!' yelled Deacon. He stopped struggling and looked up into the eyes of the soldier who had his life in his grasp. He looked calm. 'You're right, Mitch,' he said. 'It's over.'

And then he began to slowly undo the clips of his body armour.

'Oh no you don't!' roared Mitch, but he could feel the weight on his arm beginning to shift.

Suddenly the figure of Tug dropped past Mitch on a rope. His fist smashed into Deacon's face, and the assassin went limp. Tug clamped his arms around Deacon and shouted, 'Gotcha.'

27

Mitch lay on the roof, recovering his breath. The unconscious body of Deacon lay nearby. Mitch sat up and looked at Tug, coiling the length of rope.

'You made that jump without breaking a leg?' Mitch asked them, gesturing at the drop and the gap between the two roofs.

'Of course,' said Tug.

'How's Gaz?' asked Mitch.

'He's OK. The medicos are on their way to deal with him. And with you.' He watched Mitch wince in pain. 'Broken ankle?' he asked.

'I think so,' nodded Mitch. 'How are the others?'

'Everyone's fine,' said Tug. 'Most of the attackers are dead.'

'Koman?' asked Mitch.

'One broken leg, the other just torn up,' the Captain replied.

Mitch heard a loud whirring noise approaching. Looking up he saw lights in the sky.

'Helicopter,' said Tug. 'Gerald must have called in the reinforcements. Bit late if you ask me. But at least they'll be able to get you to another hospital.'

'What's wrong with the hospital we were in?' asked Mitch.

Tug looked uncomfortable. 'The place got shot up quite a bit,' he said. 'They say it's going to need some repairs before it's up and running again. Ceilings shot down. Bullet holes in the walls. Power generator blown up.' He grinned. 'Still, nothing major.'

Mitch watched the helicopter coming down towards the roof of the hospital, and then disappear from his view as it landed to pick up Gaz. In a few moments it would be collecting him and taking him to safety. The operation was over. The prime minister was safe.

Job done.

28

Mitch and Two Moons sat in the security room in the basement of the conference centre, watching the TV screens. As well as the constantly changing images from the CCTV cameras around the building, there was a screen displaying a news channel. It was showing the gathering inside the main hall in the conference centre. The British prime minister was at the podium, addressing the presidents, prime ministers and other heads of state assembled. The picture was on mute.

'You wanna hear what he's saying?' asked Two Moons, reaching for the remote control.

'Not particularly,' said Mitch, shaking his head. 'I can tell you what it will be. The fight against terrorism, the union of world leaders against international crime, that sort of thing.'

Two Moons pressed the button, and the sound came on.

'This treaty will make the world safer in the fight against terrorism. No more will international gangsters and criminals be able to use the border of one country to escape justice in another.'

Two Moons pressed the 'mute' button again.

'Guess you're right,' said Two Moons with a sigh. 'You sure you didn't write that speech for him?'

The camera travelled away from the prime minister along the platform, showing some of the other dignitaries assembled at the conference. Then it moved to the side of the stage, where Nelson, Tug and Benny stood. They were dressed in neat civilian suits, white shirts and ties, but there was no mistaking the fact that they were there as security.

It was in their alert manner, the earpieces they wore, and the unmistakeable outline of a gun underneath their jackets.

'How come they get that job?' asked Two Moons.

'Apparently, the prime minister was so impressed with the job we did at the hospital, he insisted on Delta Unit protecting him for this conference.'

'So how come we ain't up there as well?' scowled Two Moons.

Mitch grinned and pointed to the plaster cast on his ankle, and the walking stick propped up beside Two Moons' chair.

Two Moons shook his head.

'You may be an invalid,' he said, 'I ain't.'

'Then why did the hospital issue you with a stick?' asked Mitch.

'Some stupid regulation,' grunted Two Moons. 'I can walk perfectly well without it.'

To prove his point he stood up and began to walk around the room. Just then the door opened and the rest of Delta Unit came in, including Gaz, complete with one arm in a sling. Two Moons swung round and looked at the TV screen, where the soldiers were still apparently standing on duty.

'I thought those pictures were live!' he said accusingly.

'Recording,' said Tug. 'The session ended five minutes ago and we've been released from duty.'

'So we thought we'd come down here and see how the invalids were,' said Benny.

'I was just telling Mitch, I ain't no invalid,' complained Two Moons.

'You are until the medicos give you the all clear,' said Nelson. 'And that's an order.' He strode towards the vending machine in the corner of the room. 'Any of you guys care for a cup of coffee?'

There were murmurs of assent from the others.

'So, it's all over,' smiled Gaz. 'The treaty's signed. Case closed.'

'Any news on Deacon?' asked Mitch.

Nelson frowned. 'It seems the authorities don't want him to come to trial,' he said. 'He knows too many secrets they don't want to come out in court.'

'So what are they going to do with him?' asked Mitch.

'A secure mental hospital,' said Nelson. 'Indefinitely.'

'It's the best place for him,' said Gaz.

'In Texas he'd be on Death Row,' grunted Benny. 'And it'd serve him right!'

Two Moons shook his head. 'I know he was wrong, and I'm sure as hell glad we did what we did, but I still can't believe that it's the same man who saved my life in that jungle.'

'The main thing is: we did our job,' said Nelson. 'The treaty's signed, the prime minister's alive, and so are we.'

'Damn, we're good!' grinned Two Moons. 'There ain't no other outfit as good as us!'

'We're the best!' agreed Gaz with a smile.

Mitch pushed himself up out of his chair and raised his coffee cup. 'Gentlemen, I give you a toast!' he said. 'To Delta Unit. The best there is!'

The others lifted their cups in the air in a toast.

'To Delta Unit!'

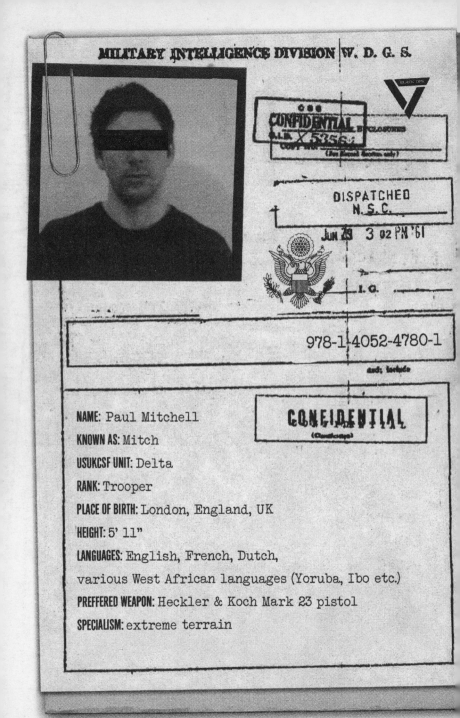

CONFIDENTIAL
X 5356

DISPATCHED
N. S. C.

JUN 29   3 02 PM '61

I. C.

978-1-4052-4780-1

CONFIDENTIAL
(Classification)

NAME: Paul Mitchell

KNOWN AS: Mitch

USUKCSF UNIT: Delta

RANK: Trooper

PLACE OF BIRTH: London, England, UK

HEIGHT: 5' 11"

LANGUAGES: English, French, Dutch,
various West African languages (Yoruba, Ibo etc.)

PREFFERED WEAPON: Heckler & Koch Mark 23 pistol

SPECIALISM: extreme terrain

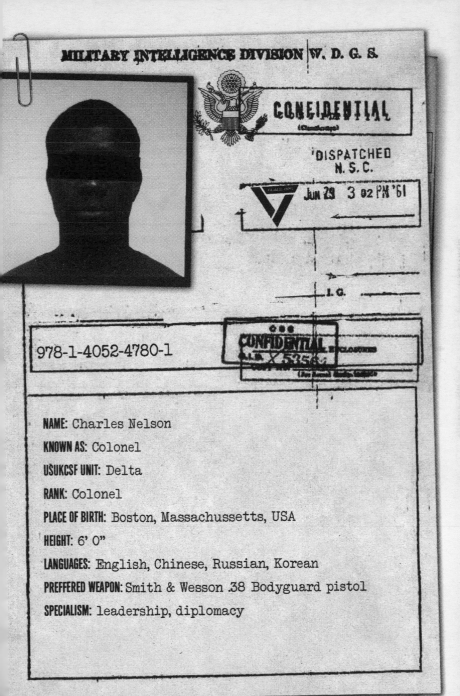

CONFIDENTIAL
(Classification)

DISPATCHED
N. S. C.

Jun 29   3 02 PM '61

I. G.

978-1-4052-4780-1

CONFIDENTIAL

NAME: Charles Nelson

KNOWN AS: Colonel

USUKCSF UNIT: Delta

RANK: Colonel

PLACE OF BIRTH: Boston, Massachussetts, USA

HEIGHT: 6' 0"

LANGUAGES: English, Chinese, Russian, Korean

PREFFERED WEAPON: Smith & Wesson .38 Bodyguard pistol

SPECIALISM: leadership, diplomacy

CONFIDENTIAL
A.I.R. X 5356

DISPATCHED
N. S. C.

JUN 29 3 02

978-1-4052-4780-1

CONFIDENTIAL
(Classification)

NAME: Tony Two Moons
KNOWN AS: Two Moons
USUKCSF UNIT: Delta
RANK: Sergeant
PLACE OF BIRTH: Arizona, USA
HEIGHT: 5' 11"
LANGUAGES: English, Inuit, Spanish, Japanese
PREFFERED WEAPON: Ingram Model 10 sub-machine gun
SPECIALISM: ordnance, explosives

NAME: Robert Tait

KNOWN AS: Tug

USUKCSF UNIT: Delta

RANK: Captain

PLACE OF BIRTH: Oxford, England, UK

HEIGHT: 5' 7"

LANGUAGES: English, Pushtu, Farsi, Hindi, Turkish

PREFFERED WEAPON: Walther P99 pistol

SPECIALISM: leadership, diplomacy

NAME: Bernardo Jaurez

KNOWN AS: Benny

USUKCSF UNIT: Delta

RANK: Lieutenant

PLACE OF BIRTH: Houston, Texas, USA

HEIGHT: 5' 7"

LANGUAGES: English, Spanish, Polish, Greek

PREFFERED WEAPON: Ruger 0.38 Service-Six pistol

SPECIALISM: tactics

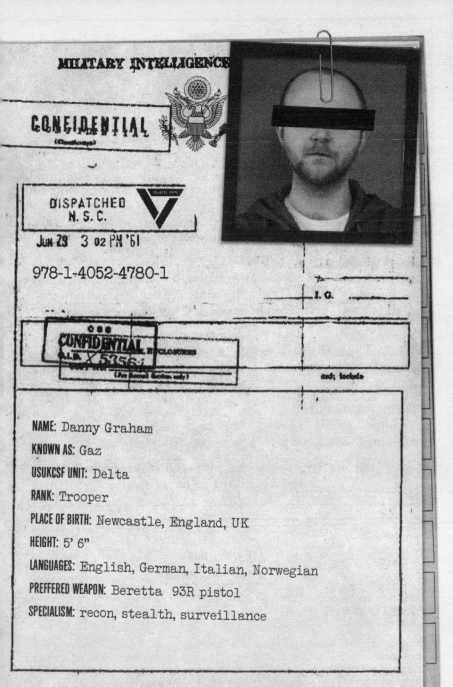

DISPATCHED
N.S.C.
BLACK OPS

Jun 29 3 02 PM '61

978-1-4052-4780-1

I.G.

CONFIDENTIAL ENCLOSURES
X 5356
(For Internal Section only)

and; include

NAME: Danny Graham

KNOWN AS: Gaz

USUKCSF UNIT: Delta

RANK: Trooper

PLACE OF BIRTH: Newcastle, England, UK

HEIGHT: 5' 6"

LANGUAGES: English, German, Italian, Norwegian

PREFFERED WEAPON: Beretta 93R pistol

SPECIALISM: recon, stealth, surveillance

EGMONT PRESS: ETHICAL PUBLISHING

Egmont Press is about turning writers into successful authors and children into passionate readers – producing books that enrich and entertain. As a responsible children's publisher, we go even further, considering the world in which our consumers are growing up.

Safety First
Naturally, all of our books meet legal safety requirements. But we go further than this; every book with play value is tested to the highest standards – if it fails, it's back to the drawing-board.

Made Fairly
We are working to ensure that the workers involved in our supply chain – the people that make our books – are treated with fairness and respect.

Responsible Forestry
We are committed to ensuring all our papers come from environmentally and socially responsible forest sources.

**For more information, please visit our website at
www.egmont.co.uk/ethical**

Egmont is passionate about helping to preserve the world's remaining ancient forests. We only use paper from legal and sustainable forest sources, so we know where every single tree comes from that goes into every paper that makes up every book.

This book is made from paper certified by the Forestry Stewardship Council (FSC), an organisation dedicated to promoting responsible management of forest resources. For more information on the FSC, please visit **www.fsc.org**. To learn more about Egmont's sustainable paper policy, please visit **www.egmont.co.uk/ethical**.